EROTIC ENCOUNTERS
OF THE CLOSE KIND

A COLLECTION OF SENSUAL SHORT
STORIES FOR WOMEN

CONTENTS

THE STORIES

DARK DESIRES: *When our two protagonists received a mysterious invitation from someone they didn't know, they should have expected the unexpected. But, not even in their wildest dreams could they have imagined what attended them behind closed doors.*

ESCAPE TO PARADISE: *Are you bored with your relationship? Have you ever thought about an illicit encounter with someone who thrills you in ways you've only ever dreamed about? Finding the time to be together and make your wildest fantasies come true can be tricky. But what if you could escape together for a few days and nights? What would you do, and who would you do it with?*

FIFTEEN MINUTES: *Isabella and I have had some interesting discussions on various aspects of erotica. In particular, voyeurism, hot wives, and the thrill that some couples get from allowing the woman to go with other men whilst her partner stays behind. And if you have yet to consider it, why not set yourselves a time limit for her to play away, say fifteen minutes, and see how it goes?*

THE UNICORN: *Is having your first bi-curious meeting an easy thing to do? It appears to be anything easy when you are a woman who wants a woman looking for a woman like you. So, when you do, make sure it's something very special for you.*

RED LETTER DAY (Flash Fiction): *Sometimes, the unexpected can be more exciting than the things you plan. And when they happen, the thrill they bring can take you to places you never imagined.*

DOWN THE STAIRS: *How do you know when you can give yourself completely to someone? By putting yourself in their hands? Trusting them to do whatever they want with you? If you really want to find out, try wearing a blindfold. It's a good place to start.*

THE GAMES PEOPLE PLAY (Flash Fiction): *What do two couples do when they lock the door behind them? Are most people strait-laced, or do they go further? And what does further really mean? How do four people, all of whom have their own individual desires, find a mutually pleasurable balance? How do they bring their fantasies together under one duvet cover?*

FLASH PHOTOGRAPHY: *Isabella has high standards on who she considers acceptable as a potential "friend with benefits". Not many potential candidates pass the test of good looks, great personality, and for men, a decent sized toolbox. Finding one is quite a challenge, but finding two who come as a package deal, what are the chances? Occasionally, Isabella strikes gold, as in this case.*

LET ME WATCH YOU: *When your lover enjoys watching you with others, what do you do? You say yes, of course.*

NEW YEARS EVE: *Cosplay is another one of those things that people do – dressing up in costume for Halloween is a good example. Perhaps you've dressed up on New Year's Eve to attend a Fancy Dress party? Maybe the event was a little racier? With all the superheroes now on our screens to choose from, which one would you choose? I know who I would want to be. Miaow!*

WAKING UP IN PARADISE: *Have you ever woken up after a night on the tiles, remembering little, if anything, of what went on? Even worse if it happens on your first night on holiday with your lover. If it happened to you, would you be shocked to discover that you* *were capable of a lot more than you had ever imagined? The most important thing is to be sure that your lover loves you just the way you are – and maybe, just maybe, if you are as bad as you can be, he will love you even more.*

PLAN A: *Sometimes you have to put yourself in the back seat when you have a friend in need. And if that literally means sitting in the back seat of a car while your friend rides in the front, then that's a sacrifice you're just going to have to make, at least until you get home.*

FIRST TIME LOVER: *In reality, a first encounter is not always as memorable as you might hope. But, with a bit of forethought and a good deal of preparation, it is also true that sometimes the first time can be truly amazing.*

THE INTERVIEW: *Being a woman of impeccable taste, I find myself attracted to men of a particular type who combine quintessentially good looks, a refined dress sense, and, most importantly, a commanding presence. My good luck in finding them and my consequential inability to resist going too far too quickly with them, regardless of who might be there too, is legendary not only within my circle of intimate friends but more widely too. So, my first day at work was always going to be more than any other day.*

THE TIME CAPSULE: *Imagine a future when you can correct past mistakes simply by swallowing a pill – a little red time capsule - and returning back to change the course of history. But what if it's not a mistake you want to fix but to make something even better?*

SOME THINGS NEVER CHANGE: *In the near future, when robots and artificial intelligence are as commonplace as singing Swedish avatars and smartphones are today, how much is likely to change beyond recognition, and how much will stay the same, or almost?*

BE CAREFUL WHAT YOU WISH FOR: *This is the story of another life in another universe, where our two protagonists meet for the first time, and their worlds collide. Just when you think you are in control of your life, something or someone comes along who throws everything up in the air.*

INTRODUCTION

This collection of short stories is an opportunity to try out ideas that might eventually merit a longer work. It does mean the occasional repetition of themes. Still, I hope there is enough variety in the narratives to entertain readers.

Whilst the stories are not written in chronological order, several maintain a familiar main character, Isabella. Similarly, whilst they don't fall into a particular category of erotica, one might argue that there are hotwife and voyeuristic undercurrents to several.

One of the aspects of the short story genre that I enjoy is that it allows readers to extend the adventure using their imagination. To this end, many stories leave me wanting more. I hope they leave a similar desire in you and open fresh avenues for exploration within your thoughts and perhaps even in the real world.

As you, the reader, peruse the pages of this book, I would love to hear your thoughts on the subject matter and your ideas for storylines you would enjoy reading about. The second volume will undoubtedly be shaped as much by your preferences as by the continuing adventures that Isabella and I look forward to sharing together.

MJ Brooke

London - October 2022

DARK DESIRES

When Isabella and Zach received a mysterious invitation from someone they didn't know, they should have expected the unexpected. But, even in their wildest dreams could they not have imagined what attended them behind closed doors. This is Isabella's version of events.

CHAPTER ONE

Walls carved from the stone of nearby cliffs rose before us, soaring up toward the sky. We held our breath, hand in hand, having climbed the weather-worn steps to the mansion. Before us towered an imposing doorway, the final barrier to whatever lay waiting inside. Beyond this archway, the unknown attended if we decided to cross over the threshold.

Our journey to this place had been anything but by accident. Our online research into libertarian pastimes, and the active pushing of our boundaries, had somehow brought us to this moment in time. We were willing, excited, and nervous - two kindred spirits on a shared voyage of sexual exploration.

We didn't know the identity of the organisers and had only recently discovered the event's location. We guessed that such events were organised in secret locations by a person or persons unknown. In all likelihood, someone we had spoken to online had recommended us. Of course, there were rumours about such gatherings, but nobody seemed to know anything for sure. Only when the invitation was delivered to us anonymously, through our door, did we have proof that these things were real. Regardless of how it came about, we found ourselves opening an envelope addressed to us both, not knowing, in the first instance, what it contained.

Gold-coloured ink on expensive ruby red writing paper, the invitation provided only the scarcest of details. We would receive the location by phone on the day of the event. Then, we were to make our way to a place in the middle of nowhere, a long way from our home, and wait for further instructions. The dress code specified the style, colour, and quality. Venetian masks were de rigueur on arrival. Removing them would result in immediate expulsion from the party, just you, not your partner. There was one further instruction: anonymity and privacy were absolute: we could never speak of the invitation, the location, or what went on inside, ever.

We gathered our thoughts, compared notes, and spent the next few days discussing the unexpected invitation. Our excitement was palpable, as was our nervousness as time passed. The prospect of stepping into the unknown was unlike anything we had ever done before. Yet, as thrilling as it might seem, we had nothing to go on, not the slightest inclination of what we might find. Even so, we felt compelled to follow through. The sexual tension and our curiosity had gotten the better of us. We waited impatiently as the days passed, our anticipation growing all the time.

CHAPTER TWO

To pass the time, we threw ourselves into online research, looking for outfits to wear. It was quite a challenge, given the dress code outlined. Eventually, we found a few niche boutiques that specialised in the look we needed. We caught an early train into the City, spending most of the day visiting every shop on our list. When the time to head home, we were still empty-handed, unable to make up our minds. We decided on a return trip the following weekend once we'd digested what we'd seen and agreed on the best attire. Decisions, it seems, were a lot harder when so much seemed to be at stake. Although we'd left empty-handed, we soon agreed on what we liked best. And so, our second trip had a much better outcome. With clear ideas, we made our choices, returning home pleased with our purchases. As an added benefit, our flirtatious behaviour throughout the day resulted in a night of love-making that reached new heights of immodesty.

After much impatient waiting, the appointed day arrived. We woke up earlier than usual, and neither of us could hide the nervous excitement that had been steadily building inside. We were thrilled and beyond nervous as we readied ourselves to step into the unknown. We remained close to each other that morning, keeping each other occupied. And the clock crept forward slowly, one long second at a time.

That afternoon we spent the better part of two hours pampering and preparing ourselves. It is curious how much effort people put into occasions that have a special meaning, even when that meaning is uncertain. And, we had no certainties of what to expect, except that we'd face it together.

We stood face-to-face, assessing and admiring each another. Our masks suited us well - black and silver for him, gold and burgundy for me, as they reflected the colour of our hair. Somehow, this felt like the first time we had been out together. And, in some ways, it was. We set out as dusk approached, climbed into our spotlessly valeted car, and headed off toward the unknown.

Our Venetian masks were a subtle but effective disguise, hiding our identities, though we could still recognise each other by the clothes we were wearing. After stopping at the mid-point for further directions, we eventually arrived at our destination, parking beside several other cars, walking the final few yards through the courtyard and up the weather-work steps, stopping only when we reached the main entrance. With no one outside and no indication of where to go, we were unsure how to announce ourselves other than knocking on the door. That seemed like the wrong thing to do, given the cloak-and-dagger nature of the invitation.

Before we could decide what to do, the entrance doors began to ease apart; two men, wearing masks and both naked to the waist, opened them for us, and then stood aside. They gestured with a slightly dramatic flourish of their free hands for us to enter, and without a word, we stepped inside. Our first glimpse of the place was of a vast atrium adorned with antique furnishings and doors leading off on all sides. The entrance closed behind us, and the fading daylight outside was extinguished like the last breath of a dying flame.

At last, we were inside the gilded cage. As far as we could see, we may have been the first to arrive. There were no other guests in the large reception area. We waited as, first, our invitation was examined and then our coats, bags, and phones were taken for safekeeping. Meanwhile, two stunning women in very revealing attire entered the hall from one of the doorways and approached us. We held each other's hands, exchanging silent glances, wondering what would happen next.

CHAPTER THREE

Beautiful, blonde, with their faces also hidden by masks, the two women stood side by side, their dresses complimentary, leaving just enough to the imagination. They observed us at length, before exchanging a few quiet words. Then, apparently having made their choice of partner, they took us by the hand, separating us and, from that moment, we both found ourselves on different paths. Unprepared for this kind of scenario, we looked over our shoulders at each other as our new companions ushered us through different doors and into separate worlds. We were no longer a couple.

I entered the room, leaving Zach to his own destiny, divided as we had been by our hosts. It was a much smaller space than the entrance hall, only dimly lit by candlelight, and the air was scented with Jasmine. I looked around, trying to take in the view. An enormous brass bath occupied the centre of the room and was filled to near overflowing with hot water and foam. Two more men, this time completely naked except and wearing masks, stood unmoving beside the bathtub. The decadence of the place was evident in the flamboyance of the furnishings. And whilst I no longer had my own man by my side, I somehow still felt completely safe. The calm demeanour of my female companion gave me with the reassurance I needed. I opened my mouth to speak, but before I could say a word, she gestured with a finger to her lips for me to stay silent. I acquiesced. By nature, I prefer being sexually passive and relaxed as she came closer until we stood mere inches apart.

Without a word, she began to undress me. I did nothing to resist, nor did I want to. The room, the settings, and the presence of their bodies, triggered a reflex desire inside, and I felt a sexual tension growing between my thighs. I was indulging myself; the unexpected loss of my partner in crime fading rapidly. One at a time, she removed my clothes and lay them on the floor under the watchful eyes of the two men nearby. I could see their physical interest in me growing. And as their excitement grew, so too did mine, the anticipation arousing my whole being.

My clothes fell away without resistance as she unzipped my dress, undid my suspender belt, careful removed my stockings, and finally freed me from my lingerie. All three of them gazed upon my naked curves. Then, retaking my hand, she assisted me as I climbed into the bath. The heat of the water caressed my skin as I entered, first one foot, then the other. I descended gently until my breasts cupped the water's edge, and I was neck deep, arching my body in response to the heat. My sexual tension rose at the thought of these strangers watching me. My nipples beginning to tighten in anticipation of what they might have planned for me next.

I didn't expect what happened next, as one of the men approached my blonde companion and undressed her with the same consummate ease she had demonstrated on me. I had the perfect front-row view of her body as he peeled away her clothes, one layer at a time.

I sensed they had done this many times before as he repeated the moves she had made with me, offering her his hand and assisting her into the bath. She entered slowly, her body facing mine. Only then did I realise how similar she and I were in so many ways - our hair, curves, and height. Only our masks hid any differences there might have been in our looks.

She lapped the soapy water over her body, between her breasts, keeping her eyes on mine. I hesitated a moment before gathering that I should follow her lead. As I did so, she leaned forward slightly, caressed her arms and legs, before reaching across to touch mine. Still silent, our bodies edged closer together, she towards me, and me towards her. We slowly became entwined, holding each other tight, in a warm, almost loving embrace. Her eyes melted any residual doubt in my mind, moulding it into desire, and our lips came together to share a long, languid kiss. I had never held a woman so tight - the scented water lapping gently against our bodies as we pressed our naked bodies together, fingers and tongues exploring each other's deepest secrets, above and beneath the waves.

I barely noticed the water flowing down my back, taken as I was by the intensity of what we were doing to each other. Then I saw her male companion, pouring water over her, and the same was happening to me. And once our backs glistened with hot, scented water, two pairs of strong hands came to rest upon our shoulders. Like a mirror, I watched her receive an exquisite massage as I received the same. Leaning forward, I was able to get a better view of her masseur, now fully aroused. His muscular arms and skilful hands pressed firmly into her shoulders, and she closed her eyes. I did the same, as his counterpart repeated the same moves on me. My body was dampened no less from the water than from the emotions now flowing freely between my legs. I confess I had no thoughts as to where my previous companion might be.

Minutes passed as the two of us gave in to the attention both men were giving us. Then, as we silently wished for more, they let go, before coming around until each was by our side. They stood beside us at a perfect height for us to reach out and take their hold of their stiff cocks. The soapiness of our hands turned their shafts into glistening trophies. And even though I wasn't usually a great fan of fellatio, tonight I was hungry and wanted to satisfy. I leaned forward and took him into my mouth, taking him as far as I could. He tasted like nothing I'd taken before. The scent of jasmine giving him a taste that was simply divine.

For a moment, I became distracted as the thought of all the time I'd invested into researching techniques to please men was about to pay off. My moves worked well on him. His breathing deepened, and he tightened his stance as I worked his shaft into my mouth while making the most of his deliciously firm butt with my free hand.

My colleague was equally adept, and both men were on the edge of oblivion within a few minutes. Then, with my goal clearly in sight, I took him deep, squeezing hard for good measure. That last move broke the proverbial camel's back, and the resulting explosion almost choked me; he had so much to give. I tried to hold on to as much as possible, but he was buried deep in my throat, and I confess to swallowing most. When he finally relented and withdrew, I let what remained of his warm juice escape from my lips, savouring the taste on my tongue. My lookalike followed moments behind, her mouth overflowing as the other man came. We shared a look of mutual satisfaction before kissing each other again, combining our hard-earned spoils in a sticky embrace.

The afterglow lasted quite a while as we remained embraced until the task of cleaning ourselves was complete, one lazy lick at a time. Then we lay back, relaxing for a while until, eventually, my companion gestured that it was time to leave our deliciously damp haven. And though the evening had just begun, I had already felt the first flushes of delight.

Attended this time by both men, we stood in the bath, our bodies glistening with moisture and satisfaction. Their modesty, now assured by white robes, they assisted me in stepping from the tub and proceeded to towel me dry. Then they gathered my clothes and helped me dress. The scene that had just unfolded echoed in my mind. I would rewind and replay those memories in the days and weeks ahead, alone in my room, free from unwanted distractions.

CHAPTER FOUR

Hand under arm once more, my bathing companion opened the door through which we had entered what seemed like a lifetime ago and ushered me through. We left the heady scent of one room behind us before entering another, this one filled with a more intense incense-laden atmosphere. The room was no more than a dozen paces long and wide, with deep, velvet seating from a bygone era carefully arranged in a wide circle. Antique light fittings flickered intermittently, providing little light, their shadows dancing on ruby-red walls. It was picture-postcard Victorian in style.

At first glance, I noticed two items out of character with the rest of the room - one hanging from the ceiling, and its companion, fixed robustly to the floor. I took a sharp intake of breath.

My guide led me to the circle's centre and squeezed my arm as a signal to stop. I looked around, holding my breath, my arms resting still by my sides. I stood just between the rings fixed to the floor and ceiling. She moved slowly behind me, hands on my waist and eyes on mine. My head turned to follow her until I could turn it no more. Her hands ran softly along my hips, over my waist, and then followed the curve of my spine until she reached my shoulders. After pausing for a moment, she took hold of the zip on my dress and pulled it down until it reached the nape of my buttocks - the end of the line. Hands once more on my shoulders, she slipped the dress from my body, revealing my black and red lace lingerie and seamed stockings held in place by suspenders. She kneeled to gather my dress, and

I stepped out before returning my feet to where they had been. I stood centre stage in the room, waiting for the audience to arrive.

My eyes grew accustomed to the dim lighting, now seeing the leather cuffs tied to bars and chains beneath my feet and above my head. My companion continued kneeling, restraining my legs, one at a time, ensuring they were well spread. I turned as best I could but could only see her shapely breasts. She shifted her position and faced me, her eyes once more on mine. We were the same height. Then, she raised my arms and strapped my wrists to the restraints hanging from the ceiling. I was now her prisoner and a captive of my unspoken desires.

I stood there, unable to do little more than observe, as she took my head in her hands and kissed me tenderly, pressing her lips to mine. Then, reaching across, she picked up a black satin hood and placed it over my head, extinguishing what little dim light there already was, leaving me in the dark. She backed away from me with a final caress, fading into the background. I was utterly alone, but not, as it transpired, for very long.

CHAPTER FIVE

Footsteps on the floor told me that others were entering the room. I couldn't be sure how many, with too few voices and too many similar sounds. Though I couldn't determine what they were saying, both women and men were in the crowd. Little by little, I heard them taking their seats. It's strange how your other senses kick in when you cannot see. Like the moment at the theatre when the audience seats itself before the performance starts, I was centre stage, the star of the show, but I hadn't read the script. And then the room fell silent.

I could smell the musky odour of skin, and it was enough to tell me who was there. Four warm, strong hands touched my body, running over my naked flesh. A shiver ran down my spine as I thought of the two men who had earlier helped me bathe. I could still taste the fruits of my labour, salty on my lips. My legs spread wide and held firmly by restraints were no defence against what they had in mind. One in front of me and the other behind, they took hold of my knickers and dragged them forcefully down, exposing me to unknown eyes. Their descent halted above my knees, unable to go any further, the spread of my legs resisting the fabric as it stretched. It was as far as my underwear would go, but only the beginning of where these two would go.

I felt their lips and tongues advance on me: a pincer movement, front and rear. I was defenceless. As wonderful as it had been before to take them into my mouth, this was something else. Now, their tongues delved into my deepest, most intimate spaces. My uninvited audience began to voice their pleasure.

Now attuned to the darkness, I heard the audience as they disrobed, adjusting their position to accommodate one another, undoubtedly for their mutual satisfaction. My mind's eye filled in the rest.

And deeper they went, my two lovers, hidden from my eyes, satiating their hunger. Then, their fingers came into play. First one, then the other, as they explored their willing captive. And all around, the whispers grew to moans. They all came, saw, and came once more.

Having completed their initial exploration, my two invaders retreated momentarily, leaving me hanging. And then they moved in. Their bodies pressed against mine – one in front, the other behind. I could feel their arousal nestled within my curves. Their kisses opened my floodgates - lips and tongues, exploring every inch of my aching body. On and on they went as the music in my mind raced towards its obvious conclusion.

And then the shackles holding my ankles somehow fell away. By design, no doubt, though I could not see. My legs freed once more; they removed my knickers, the last obstruction to their ultimate goal. And gravity took them to the ground.

The benefit of having my wrists bound became apparent as I held on tight and was lifted clean from the floor. One man hooked my legs and pulled them around his waist. His cock took no prisoners as I welcomed it into me. I grasped the bar above my wrists as his hands took hold of my waist. He drove as deep as he could, easing my thighs back and forth, and I closed my blindfolded eyes in response. His size and angle were new to me. I was in no position to resist what came next, though resistance was the last thing on my mind.

Two more hands took my thighs from behind, easing apart my cheeks. I recalled how stiff these two had been and waited for the inevitable. Wet as I was, his firm cock entered me easily from behind. They filled me beyond my wildest dreams, and I could hardly breathe. And then, the sweetest moment, as they removed the hood from my eyes. I took in the view. It was unlike anything I had ever imagined. I was naked, being taken by these two incredible men, whilst my audience, in various stages of undress, was inspired by my performance to follow my lead.

My legs were held by one, my thighs by the other, suspended in mid-air, as they pushed and pulled together. I held on as long as I could, not wanting the feeling to stop. Until I could resist no more, abandoning myself to waves of pleasure flooding my whole body. They sensed my moment coming and chose not to deny themselves. They held on as long as they could until I shook with uncontrollable desire. They released into my body, filling me to overflow. Then they held me there. Their cocks plugged me tight as long as they could, and when they finally slipped out, two fountains of cum followed, escaping down my legs and my ass. And we rested together, their pleasure as measurable as mine.

Finally, they released me from my binds, and I fell between my lovers, exhausted but deeply satisfied. And, as I rested, my thoughts drifted to where and what my companion was doing. My first thought for him all night. Where was he? What had he done? Well, that is a story for another time.

ESCAPE TO PARADISE

Are you bored with your relationship? Have you ever thought about an illicit encounter with someone who thrills you in ways you've only ever dreamed about? Finding the time to be together and make your wildest fantasies come true can be tricky. But what if you could escape together for a few days and nights? What would you do, and who would you do it with?

CHAPTER ONE

Surprise!

How Zach managed to keep it a secret from me, I don't know. I adored the way he organised surprises for me. I just love a man who tries. Even so, when I opened his latest "My darling Isabella" email and saw he'd booked tickets for three balmy nights in September at the most expensive, up-market, swanky hotel in Ibiza, my heart skipped a beat. The thought of spending all that time together made me tingle. Half a second later, the sensible part of my brain – albeit in a minority since he and I had first met – sounded alarm bells. With all our work and complicated personal lives, I wondered how we would manage three nights away.

At this point, I should mention that we are lovers, with all the passion that comes from two people who have found their perfect other half, even if only for stolen moments, far away from the madding crowd and unsuspecting spouses.

But I digress. It was clear that Zach had planned everything down to the last detail. He had conjured up a makeshift website, publicising a business conference in Ibiza that week, giving us the excuse we both needed to escape to the sun. I liked that he was hunky and geeky – a cocktail mix of nine parts James Bond and one part Q, shaken, not stirred. The perfect blend. Okay, I know, Q just came out as gay, but that's the concession I must give Zach anyway for being in touch with his feminine side – his three per cent, as he calls it. Just as long as he doesn't change the blend, or I'll start getting jealous of the guys he talks to, as well as taking him to task whenever girls approach him, which I am pleased to say, is quite often. Even though he's in his late forties, just like me, he looks and feels like a man half his age – yum-yum!

Two days later and everyone in my book club was in the know. I couldn't stop myself from sharing our little secret, and the group was nothing else, if not the perfect place to confide in scandals and gossip. Of course, the ladies demanded photos of Zach on the beach. The guys asked me to send them live-streaming videos from our bedroom - typical men.

Since we first met a couple of years ago, through one of those sites for close encounters of the illicit kind, we'd made sexy new friends, and there were more in the book club. Even though we'd only met them for drinks and late-night banter, my revelation about Ibiza meant Zach and I were officially the main talking point for the group until September finally arrived. I had my suitcase packed with all the essentials for three nights of beachside and bedside fun. I waited impatiently for my Uber driver to come and whisk me to the airport, where Zach was punctual as always and waiting for me at the airport, looking at his watch. Two female flight attendants were in deep conversation with him. I reminded myself not to leave him alone for a moment whilst we were away.

I had packed enough sexy clothing to last a month and stashed my little bag of fun-time toys under layers of lacy lingerie. The thought of an airport security guard rummaging through my hand luggage and examining them one by one might have been embarrassing to others. Still, I got turned on by the possibility of a sexy security guard frisking me. If only! I couldn't wait to get him – my man, not the security guard – all to myself in a hot tub or on the beach. Watch out Ibiza, here we come!

CHAPTER TWO

On Arrival

What was there not to love about the hotel, or our room, a ground-floor suite with a private pool? The main gathering space was terrific. It was a luxurious locale with classy high stools running the length of the bar. I made a mental note of them as Zach had a "thing" about bar stools. He had a fantasy about me sitting at the bar in a locale just like this, and I imagined that this was one of the reasons he'd chosen this place.

As well as splendid views of the beach, the hotel had an outdoor nightclub, a fabulous swimming pool, hot tubs in every room, and a communal sauna which were just part of the all-inclusive package, as were the food and drinks. Best of all, it was for adults only – no under-eighteens winding up the grown-ups, and lots of fun-loving adults partying at night. So, all that was left to do was to unpack, chill out in the hot tub, and then dress to thrill later that evening. At least, that was the plan.

As chance would have it, things started to get interesting just an hour or two after checking in. Zach reckons we have this magical ability to make every situation naughty by our mere presence. Call it our magnetism, but wherever we go, people just seem, well, horny. I think he gets up to mischief and ensures I'm there when it happens.

On our arrival, I did my usual thing and posted a couple of pictures on Instagram. The typical frisky comments came straight back from a couple of girls from the book club. They were trying to get me to ramp up my normal flirtatious behaviour a notch or two, and I was happy to give them what they wanted. I called Zach into the hot tub as quickly as possible so I could send them images of him beaded with sweat. I could only imagine what the two of them would be getting up to with those photos to hand.

Photoshoot completed, we left behind the hot tub, showered, and slid beneath the soft sheets covering the most oversized bed I had ever had the pleasure to occupy. With my legs apart, Zach weighed down upon me, his lips and fingers exploring every inch of my willing body.

I was in heaven. Well, I was until the moment there came a knock on the door. We'd ordered champagne to celebrate but had got distracted waiting for it to arrive. I looked at Zach as he lay on top of me and caught him looking at me with a twinkle in his eyes. I felt him throb inside of me. What was he getting up to now? I grew moist. Anticipation is a wickedly delicious emotion, and I was on high alert.

Zach rolled over as if he were getting up to answer the door. Instead, his hand reached out and swooped up my black negligee from the floor where I'd dropped it earlier. He passed it across to me, turning back toward me with that oh-so-innocent voice he used at times like this. He asked if I minded finding out who was at our door as he was still "too aroused" to do so. I gave him my standard "you bad boy" look, but he smiled and protested his innocence. He had me where he wanted me.

Barely covering my curves, I draped the negligee around me and placed my feet firmly on the floor. Then, stomping in fake indignation, I made for the door, opening it timidly. If Zach knew who was behind the door, he didn't show it. Standing in front of me was the hottest guy I had seen in a long time – Zach apart, of course – tanned and toned, with a pair of crystal glasses and a bottle of champagne balanced perfectly on the tray he held with one hand. I yanked the door open so quickly that my negligee flew apart for an instant. It was enough to make his gaze fall swiftly from my face to my legs, and his expression turned to desire. I swear I saw his crotch throb too. We stood there, unmoving, and silent, for what seemed like forever. He looked like he was memorising every curve of my body. I, in turn, studied his name badge: Luca.

Having regained his composure, Luca thrust the tray towards me. I held back a smile as he seemed almost embarrassed. Instead, I chose to tease him just a little more. I bit my lip, giving him one of my sexy "I would love to fuck you" looks before reaching out to take the tray. He relinquished his grasp just a little too slowly, keeping his eyes on me all the time. I knew Zach was enjoying watching the show I was putting on, as much for his pleasure as my own.

I turned back into the room, thanking Luca as I flicked the door closed with a swish of my thigh, hoping he seized the chance to see my gorgeous ass as I did so. That was fun, and I got more turned on than when he'd first knocked on the door. I returned to Zach, still lying there smiling, his hand strategically positioned, even stiffer than when I'd left him. A naughty thought crossed my mind. Was there a limit on the times I could call for room service? Well, I had lots of lingerie and only three days to try everything out.

We opened the bottle of champagne and toasted our arrival in style. I let my mind drift to Luca as my leading man filled me up and made me come. I was behaving like a bad girl. I knew it, and Zach knew it. I wondered if Luca knew it too. I wanted him to find out.

CHAPTER THREE

The First Night

Oops, I'd forgotten my toothbrush! That is typical of me. It had been a running joke since the first time we spent the night together when I'd forgotten to pack it. We ended up experimenting with his multi-function, pulsating, vibrating toothbrush in many ways, all of which were guaranteed to invalidate the warranty.

The hotel was breath-taking, as I've already said. The guests were classy and more attractive than your average four-star guests, and from what I could gather, they seemed an exciting bunch. The hotel's ambience was enchanting and subtly sensual, from the décor in the rooms to the bar's layout, with deep, burgundy-red, leather sofas and expensive thick pile carpet. Then there was the hotel personnel, looking as if they had auditioned for Love Island. It was enough to make you shiver but in a good way.

Come nine o'clock, we readied ourselves and decided to dress up for the evening. By the time we'd finished, we both looked like porn actors attending an award ceremony. Zach suited a black-tie tuxedo. It was enough to make me feel like taking him there and then, but when he pulled out a pair of diamond earrings to compliment my stunning outfit (his words, not mine), I forgot about sex and decided to put them on. I have my priorities. Diamonds always come first.

The food, wine, and conversation were delightful. Afterwards, we headed to the bar and found a couple of bar stools that gave us the best view of our surroundings. Imagine a room glittering with gold and dark red fittings, sensual music in the background, and beautiful people talking, laughing, and having fun. We spent the first half an hour playing our favourite game – people-watching. With lots to watch and even more to discuss and debate, the conversation flowed easily.

After two cocktails, we had both moved up a gear into flirt mode. His fingers toyed with the abundant flesh on show, given my skimpy dress. Shivers ran up and down my spine as his fingers lingered between my thigh and my lace holdups. His meanderings didn't go unnoticed as many of the guests – clearly people watchers themselves – enjoyed the show we were putting on.

As the bar filled with clientele, we spent the next hour or so in polite conversation with couples that came and went and got to know the bar staff. They understood that friendly conversation and overfilling drinks translated into sizeable tips. We even discovered that Luca – the room service guy – also worked behind the bar. He had a great deal of stamina, pulling double shifts - just the kind of stamina a girl likes to see.

As the evening turned to night-time, everyone began drifting outdoors. There the dance floor merged seamlessly with the hotel's secluded beach. The late summer heat and the salty scent of the ocean mingled together, giving the place a taste of paradise. The low-key, rhythmic music pulsated. It was not the kind of club music we had expected. Instead, it was almost hypnotic as people danced at very close quarters.

I checked my messages, including two from girlfriends enjoying their party back home with a couple of guys they'd gotten to know at a local bar. They were sharing photographs of their underwear flying across the room. I noticed they were both wearing red knickers and little else. I told them they were both very, very bad. They sent me two kisses and three banana emojis in reply.

My phone rang, and I had to take the call. My sister was checking in with me. Taking the opportunity, Zach stood up and excused himself – something about freshening up. He kissed my cheek and headed for the door. Out of the corner of my eye, I caught him briefly exchanging words with two guys we had met earlier before he continued on his way. I turned my attention back to my sister, assuring her that I was having a wonderful time and not to worry, confirming that there were hot men in abundance. Minutes later, we said goodnight, and I stashed my phone, looking up for the first time since the start of the conversation. I was surprised at who was there, right in front of me, just waiting to meet my gaze.

CHAPTER FOUR

Party Time

The two guys who'd had a brief conversation with Zach were sitting directly opposite me on one of those fabulous burgundy-red, leather sofas scattered throughout high-class bars. No big deal, you'd think. The only thing is, they were both looking straight into my eyes. Still no big deal? Well, sitting sandwiched between the two of them was a stunning older woman – I found out later her name was Jade – sporting jet black hair, piercing blue eyes, a pearl necklace highlighting her long neck, and the shortest of red dresses, which worked on her thanks to a pair of slender legs that went on and on. She wore heels that even I would have struggled to walk in. And I don't need to tell you where her hands were. She was stroking between their legs as if they were two pussies. Their jackets were wide open, black ties undone. Both of them leaned back into the deep sofa. They were unashamedly purring with the loving attention she was giving them – smack in the centre of the room!

It took considerable effort for me to regain my composure. It felt like I had a front-row seat to the opening scene of a porn movie. I briefly scanned the room, searching for Zach. He headed my way, taking long slow steps, seemingly pleased with himself. My eyes flicked back to the two guys on the sofa, still enjoying the attention they were receiving. Okay, enough, Isabella; behave, I told myself. I returned my gaze to Zach. He had a twinkle in his eyes – the same one he'd had earlier when Luca – he of room service – had knocked on our hotel door. My insides fluttered.

Something about that look of his made me wet in anticipation. Whatever Zach was getting up to, it always involved me front and centre. Ha, I just thought – front and centre – such fitting words. But that's a story for later.

We sat together on our bar stools and, given the show being put on for our attention, we took our people-watching skills to the next level, watching, and commenting on the three of them having fun on the sofa. My hand found itself resting on his upper thigh. I felt a giveaway throb from time to time as his eyes met hers, and we followed the scene unfolding before our eyes. We fell silent as the show became hotter, enjoying the elegance of her hand movements until Zach leant across and whispered in my ear, making me instantly gush. He'd noticed how the two guys were still looking right at me, despite the attention they were getting from Jade.

We were pulled back to reality as Luca – yes, him – approached and asked if we wanted a refill. Of course, the room service man had become our personal bar serviceman. Lucky me! Our drinks cut two lonely figures having been consumed and discarded, and he was back to see if I needed filling up again. Uh-oh, my body was dealing with too many flutters today. His fit, tanned body and muscular arms were having an undeniably delicious effect on me. I think it was the effect he desired too.

We ordered two more Marguerites, ready to step down from our bar stools and head to the adjacent dance area outside. I thought a little fresh air might cool me down, having just spent the last half hour being turned on by all the hot guys – mine included – paying me so much attention. So, what's a girl to do? Unfortunately, I soon learned that fresh air and cooling down don't go together.

As I was gathering my things, Zach reached into his breast pocket and handed something to Luca. I knew we had a fully inclusive package and wondered why Zach paid for our drinks. Ha! As if that was what was on his mind. I should have joined up the dots.

He leaned across to Luca and whispered something in his ear which, despite my best endeavours, I didn't catch. Their eyes met; Luca nodded and headed toward the end of the bar, slipping whatever Zach had given him into his trouser pocket. A tip, I thought. Still, my eyes followed him as he stepped away from behind the bar and turned toward me. As he came closer, his hand returned to his pocket, and I caught him pulling something out. Whatever it was, it glimmered in the light. He headed straight toward me with intent. My heart skipped a beat.

As he reached us, I finally recognised the object he was holding. The thing Zach had given him. Really? You bad boy, Zach. My precious bejewelled backdoor toy held firmly in Luca's sexy, suntanned hand. I was getting nervous and excited in equal measure. No, scrub that. I was utterly soaked by this point. With a helping hand from Zach, I stepped down from the bar stool. My high heels landed at ground zero, and my short skirt slipped first up as I rose, then down again as I descended. What was going on? My head was spinning, and the butterflies were having a field day.

Zach took my hands and placed them on his shoulders without giving me time to think or react. He put his hands around my waist and took a small step back, making me lean ever so lightly forwards, my butt jutting out at an angle. I took a long hard look at him, one of my what-are-you-up-to looks. I caught the two guys on the sofa out of the corner of my eye. They were now enjoying watching what was happening between me Zach, and

Luca, right before their eyes. I knew what was coming as Luca moved smoothly behind me, his hands resting on my legs, just below the hemline of my dress. I froze in time and space. Zach's hands now slowly moved skywards, taking my dress with them.

Keeping time with Zach, as if they were a duo, Luca moved his hands upwards, following the seams of my holdups, past the lace edges, onto my bare thighs, and continued onwards and upwards. Finally, he reached the heady heights of my pearl-adorned, open-crotch underwear. I felt his fingers steer themselves blindfolded around the curves of my ass, searching for the doorway to my darkest recess. His fingers, wet from his searches, caressed my backside until he found the opening and gently slid them inside, easing his way in, deftly widening the path.

After what seemed like ages of toying with me but was less than a minute, I felt the cold touch of smooth, shiny metal against my skin as he worked his magic on me with the plug Zach had given him. Backdoor tightness gave way to an open invitation. I was standing, legs slightly apart, with this near stranger taking my toy and gently pushing it into me. He held it tight as it slid inwards, waiting until I had taken all of it. A final caress and his work was done, my dress adjusted, and my position returned upright once more. The operation had taken a little over thirty seconds, but my goodness, which had been the best half minute of my life – well, maybe not, but close.

I turned to thank Luca, why I'm not sure, but he was already returning to the bar. My eyes fell. I could have done with a taste of him just then. But instead, I looked back toward Zach and gave him my naughtiest smile. You must hand it to me. I had a very, very bad boy as a lover. And now it was time for a breath of fresh air. I have no idea just how I was expected to walk in a straight line.

CHAPTER FIVE

Taking It Easy

From the bar to the dance area was a matter of a dozen paces, but I had never tried to walk in high heels, a tight dress, and a toy wedged up in no-man's land. The sensation was scandalously divine – especially given how I'd found myself "plugged" in the first place - another experience to add to my "do-it-again" list. I might also have had a brief passing thought about including Luca on the "to-do" list too!

We passed the guys on the sofa with whom I'd spent part of the evening enjoying them, watching me watching them. I knew they had also been avidly soaking up the scene that had just taken place in front of them. Their excitement stood out – literally. I passed by with the merest of glances, doing my best to act nonchalantly whilst my body decided of its own volition that they were close enough to make me shudder with delight.

What was this place? It felt like nothing I'd ever experienced before. Here I was with the sexiest guy I could wish to be with, and even so, I was finding time to take in other guys with lustful desire. But my, those Marguerites must have been stronger than I realised! I needed a timeout.

I loosened my grip on Zach and signalled that I needed to freshen up. He pulled me close and kissed me the way only he knew how, a look of love and desire in his eyes. He held his gaze on my silhouette as I walked away. I love a man who pays attention to his woman.

The restroom was crowded, with women discussing this and that. Smalltalk didn't hide the fact that they were having fun. Two girls followed me in, and the one behind me couldn't resist bumping into my backside. She apologised, but not before I felt her hand slip between my cheeks, searching for the toy now firmly wedged within me. There followed a substantial "Oh my god, which was so amazing, did you see how hot he was" conversation with two of them – although I never got their names. I wasn't sure if they were referring to Zach or Luca. Either way, they would have been right. Both were hot. We swapped room numbers and air kisses before I got back to the job of freshening up. I walked out, noticing that the two girls who had seen what Luca did, had spread the news quickly to their friends, and I was the new bad girl on the block.

Back in the bar, I looked around until I found Zach. He was relaxing on yet another leather sofa at the edge of the dance area, making polite conversation with a couple sitting next to him. He looked up and stood as I approached – always the gentleman – making space for me to sit next to the woman. And then it hit me. The woman was Jade. She, who minutes earlier had been attending to the needs of the two guys on the other sofa. And now she was with another man. Not just any other man, though. This one was her partner. My mind raced in every direction. Had he just arrived? Had he seen her with those other two guys? Had he wanted to see her with those two? Maybe it was the experience I had just had, but my mind was running down a one-way track – it felt like there was something very naughty about this place, and I had found myself bang, smack in the middle.

All I could think of was that we were sitting here with another man and woman, and they both looked and smelled divine. What might happen next? What do they want? What do I want?

What does Zach want? I might have fainted!

CHAPTER SIX

You Spin Me Round

As I've already mentioned, one of my favourite pastimes is people-watching, especially when Zach is with me. The two of us, thick as thieves, were comparing notes on who was doing what, with whom, and why. The situation was very different tonight – I wasn't sure who was watching who. I felt like all eyes in the room were on us after my earlier experience. More so, with the four of us sitting snugly together on a big, burgundy-red, leather sofa, with an audience of dozens of sexy people on the dance floor. The music pulsated with a slow pounding rhythm that ran straight through my body.

Although the sofa was deep and inviting, it wasn't big enough for four people to sit together. As I found out, Jade and I were the sandwich-filling for Zach and Tom. I sat with my knees clenched, my thighs even more so, and I'd never realised how arousing it would be to feel the gentle pressure from the pearls on my knickers and my plug. Both objects were teasing me as the music sent waves of pleasure running through my body.

Our conversation moved from polite to borderline flirty, which naturally became less nuanced with every sip of our drinks as if a tap were being opened bit by bit – gradually turning into a total, uncontrollable rush of dampness.

I could feel the temperature rising; our chemistries reacting together. It became clear that our new acquaintances knew what they wanted. Unfortunately, I hadn't worked out precisely what they wanted from Zach or me.

Although slightly tipsy from the drinks, the "be well-behaved" part of my mind made one final effort to engage. Take slow, deep breaths, I told myself. Keep calm and focused. And whatever you do, sip your cocktail very, very slowly. Pep-talk over. Thank you very much, moral compass. Now, where was I? Twenty minutes and another cocktail consumed, my head was spinning delightfully, and I realised I was incapable of sipping a cocktail slowly. I was also about to find out what they planned. Not exactly what I'd expected, but then again, I love surprises.

CHAPTER SEVEN

Then There Were Five

One of the disadvantages, or advantages, depending on whether what happens next is pleasurable, is that head-spinning cocktails slow your reaction time to events going on around you. That's my excuse for what followed, and I'm sticking to it. The fact that what happened was very pleasurable is irrelevant. My defence is solid, milord. I was incapable of resisting the temptation due to one delicious cocktail too many. The fault lies with the barman.

I mention cocktails because the first time I realised that Luca was again standing in front of me was when I saw the drinks appear from nowhere on the table in front of the four of us. By this time, Jade and I had one hand on each other's thigh and the other hand on our respective men. I don't recall precisely how they got there; suffice it to say, everyone's movements were of the caressing kind. It was enough to raise the temperature by at least two degrees.

If you've ever watched one of those slow-motion moments in a movie when an object is flying towards you, then you know exactly how it felt when I saw those drinks appear. My head and eyes moved slowly up from the table, devouring Luca's tall, fit, sideways profile as he straightened up from lining up our four cocktails on the table. His eyes met mine as he turned toward me with a mischievous smile and a seductive twinkle in those big brown eyes. What is it about men I like? They've all got that twinkle. I was now pinned in on three sides by men with seductive looks.

I was about to say something when Jade's hand squeezed my thigh as she lifted herself from the sofa, eyes fixed on Luca, leaving a space between me and her partner, Tom. And just like waves that shift on the ocean, Tom adjusted his position, and within the blink of an eye, I found myself caught between him and Zach, the two of them close enough to touch me and be touched by me.

Whether or not the drinks had slowed my reflexes, I was enjoying the unexpectedness of events as they played out at pace. I had never found myself in a situation like this before, and even though it seemed like time was standing still, only moments passed between one wave of arousal and the next. I felt like I had a front-row seat in an incredible theatre or ballet production. I didn't know that I was about to become one of the show's stars.

As Jade rose from the sofa, I was given a close-up view of her gorgeous dress, short enough to allow the lace tops of her seamed holdups to peek out from behind. She had a fantastic figure – not skinny – but perfectly meandering curves for a woman who was happy with who she was. Both men beside me were doing as I was and admiring her curves.

The feedback I got from both men was the throbbing of their stiffness under my fingertips – I may have forgotten to mention where my hands had fallen – oops. Next, their hands slid gently along my legs, shifting the hem of my short dress upwards - further evidence of their and my state of mind. Then, in perfect time, their hands crossed the borders of my holdups, resting themselves between silk and flesh. My heart skipped another beat. I leaned back deep into the sofa; my eyes were half closed as I soaked up the pleasure I was feeling. I'd never really experienced the purposeful touch of two men at the same time. Still, the way they moved in unison made the sensations flood through me, dampening me even more sensual and arousing than I would have imagined.

I'm not exactly sure how it happened, as I became caught between my pleasure and watching the scene unfold, but I didn't expect what came next.

Standing in front of me, my female friend leaned forward and whispered something I didn't catch to the barman. I felt her partner throb again as she did so. A few moments later, the barman took her hand and raised it skywards. At that precise moment, she pirouetted perfectly on her high heels, spinning around to face me, her back now to the barman. She looked down from on high. A magnificent tall statue, hiding the barman from my view. My eyes moved upwards as here shifted her down until our gazes met. Her face radiated sexiness. The barman placed one hand on either side of her dress at the hemline and began pulling the sides up slowly, seductively. I'm not sure if my mouth was wide open at that point, but I'm pretty sure my pupils dilated, and my breathing became heavy with lust. I watched as her dress rose slowly but surely upwards, exposing her beautiful lace tops before reaching an expensive, deep red thong. The three of us on the sofa stared in awe at the sight unfolding before us, each of us getting more excited as the seconds passed.

In my mind, I already imagined that she might be about to receive the same kind of attention that I had gotten less than an hour earlier, although Luca had no such toy in his hand. Instead, what he was about to have in his hand was far larger than the present he had given me. I could hardly believe it as he deftly undid his trousers, easing his breathtakingly delicious manhood out. His arousal was impressive.

Without pausing for thought, holding her dress high enough to do what Jade had asked for, he slipped inside her from behind, easily avoiding the minimal protection offered by her underwear. She moaned loudly as the tip of his manhood entered her. Instantly she leant toward me, offering herself to him in a more accommodating fashion. Her hands fell squarely onto my knees. She eased herself further forward, placing the weight of her body onto my legs, staring straight into my eyes with a look of sweet desire. Luca thrust himself deep into her. Her eyes opened wide in surprise at his size. I could feel the pressure of her keeping herself in balance as she leaned on me. Then more pressure she applied to me, the more she forced my legs to spread apart. I resisted until I saw a look in her eyes, and I knew she was toying with me, inviting me to follow her lead.

Another deep thrust and she gasped out loud. Her head shot back as she enjoyed the pleasure she was receiving. Luca grabbed her long black hair with one hand and pulled her tighter. My legs were now held apart by Jade, pinned to the two men sitting at either side of me, their hands tightening their grip on my thighs, their fingers edging toward the insides of my legs, just a hairsbreadth away from my moist womanhood. For sure, the tips of their fingers were already aware of just how damp I had become as my legs widened further with every deep dive Luca made into Jades inviting body. I had a decision to make. I found a resting place for each on my hands tight around the throbbing goods of Zach and Tom. My mind was spinning from the pleasure of what I saw, what I was holding, and where I wanted both men to go. What is a poor girl to do?

CHAPTER EIGHT

Sweet Surrender

I found myself floating in a dream-like state between fantasy and reality. The clear, dark sky above, flickering with a billion tiny stars; the warm, heady sea breeze of late summer flooding my senses; the silhouettes of once strangers, now lovers, surrounding me, keeping in time with the music and the movements of our hands – theirs on my intimacy, mine on theirs. We were a combined symphony of sight, sound, and the heady scent of our bodies.

I held the gaze of Jades' beautiful blue eyes. Her face was a portrait of pure abandon. Each time she took Luca deep inside, her expression became more intense. Her lust for him, for us, was palpable. An instinctive need to be taken in the moment. No forethought, no planning, just the sense of here and now. And I felt the same need rising from deep inside. With every thrust of his beautiful, desirable body, my legs flowed ever more with desire. Any residual hesitation was abandoned as I gave myself completely to this moment and my need for satisfaction.

I burrowed into the warm, inviting sofa. My head resting against the scented leather, eyes half closed in anticipation. Jade followed my lead, shifting her weight so I could lift and raise my legs over both men, offering them – and her – an open invitation to my most intimate of places. She brought herself forward, approaching me with just one objective in mind. Her eyes shifted from my face to the men's hands, working with shared intent between my legs. Then, in perfect unison, as Zach slipped his fingers beneath the crotch of my soaking panties, pulling them to one side, Tom simultaneously positioned his fingers, damp from my desire, around my smooth, hungry edges.

He spread me apart enough for Jade to arrive just moments later. Her red lips caressed my dampness. I instinctively pushed myself towards her, the pleasure of our now physical connection growing.

I had never felt a woman's touch on my body, let alone down there. I closed my eyes with abandon as her tongue made its presence known, flicking deep within me, my body responding with a feeling of sweet surrender.

I felt the first waves of what was to come. Every fibre of my body was tense, every muscle taught. With each forceful thrust of his body, the barman pushed my female lover closer to me, the caress of her lips and tongue becoming fuller and faster with every stroke. As I floated in heaven, my hands tightened of their own accord on the clothing around both men. I held on to just enough awareness to recognise a stiffness in both their bodies I had rarely felt before. I felt ravenous, a hungry creature ready to pounce upon her prey. I wasn't going to be satisfied with one of them. I wanted them both. I wanted to feel their nakedness and the taste of their bodies - the fullness of their passion buried deep within my loins.

Perhaps they were reading my mind. Maybe we were all reading each other's minds? As if in response to my thoughts, I felt them shifting position at the same moment. How did they know what I wanted? I knew my man was deliciously bad, but could he have been so bad as to orchestrate all of this? My mind was spinning as I tried to understand how I had gotten myself into this. But my body told me I was precisely where I'd always longed to be.

I loosened my hold just long enough for them to free themselves from the captivity of their clothing before grasping their naked, throbbing cocks in my hands. My pulse was racing again. I followed the rhythm of the background music, repeatedly squeezing and relaxing my grip, stroking them in unison. Slowly at first, I increased to a fuller, more decisive motion taking them inevitably to their respective points of no return.

Just as a symphony builds to a crescendo, we reached the peak of ecstasy, a tsunami of combined pleasure. My orgasm was uncontrollably intense. My entire being was overcome with wave after wave of emotional release. My hands felt the pulsating rush of both men, simultaneously exploding over my skin – two delicious, warm showers of satisfaction, a taste of things to come.

Luca peaked moments later, sending shivers down Jades' legs as she gushed unashamedly in response to the explosion he had just unleashed inside her. Unable to control her orgasm, she sent a shower of wet desire across our bodies, completing the opera.

We collapsed in a collective heap of spent souls. Five bodies amassed together on the sofa - no clear beginning or ending to who was holding onto whom. Silence descended. In front of us, the music had quietened as if to accentuate our coming. Those on the dancefloor were looking our way. They had been our secret audience. Others, oblivious to what had just happened, were going on with their lives.

Slowly, my focus began to return. I realised I had crossed a line and didn't want to go back. I had stepped through the looking glass into a universe where the old rules didn't apply. In fact, at this precise moment, there were no rules, only my wants and desires. As I lay half naked in their midst, I didn't want to move, and I didn't want this moment to pass. All I could think of was – if this was only day one, what would tomorrow bring? I knew I would find out soon enough whether I had any rules left. Time for yet another cocktail, I thought. It was going to be a long night.

FIFTEEN MINUTES

Isabella and I have had some interesting discussions on various aspects of erotica. In particular, voyeurism, hot wives, and the thrill that some couples get from allowing the woman to go with other men whilst her partner stays behind. And if you have yet to consider it, why not set yourselves a time limit for her to play away, say fifteen minutes, and see how it goes?

CHAPTER ONE

I took a deep breath and opened the door. The party was already in full swing. Music from another era and conversation in the here and now combined to fill the air. They mixed perfectly with the heady cocktail of perfume, people, and alcohol. My arrival caused a buzz. The red outfit I had chosen was perfect for the occasion. One after another, heads turned my way. Casual glances became lingering looks. Whispered exchanges made others stop and stare. Then, just for a moment, everything went silent. Then as suddenly as it had come, the moment passed, and everyone returned to what they were doing a split instant before I arrived. My underwear dampened as strangers' eyes lingered on me. I felt special.

My escort had left me to my own devices for an allotted time. We had agreed that I would have 15 minutes exactly – not a moment more – to introduce myself into the fray. I checked my watch. I had no time to lose. This was a dream I intended to make come true.

Making my way to the bar, I spied the eyes fall upon my curves as I passed first one, then another man, woman, and couple. They all wanted a closer look at my curves, poorly concealed underneath the sexiest jacket dress I kept in my wardrobe for a special occasion. And this was one of those occasions. My stockings markedly flashed their lace edges as I took each step. I gave the coyest look I could muster as I penetrated deeper into the crowd. Bodies edging closer with each step.

I was moving in slow-motion, time almost standing still, as those few steps to the bar took forever. I took in the view. So much temptation surrounded me, and I had no idea what I might do. And then, I reached the bar.

The bartender came over, and he was a remarkable sight. My panties took another shower of uncontrolled lust. I stuttered out my order, in response to which he nodded silently with a smile that melted my insides. He had my attention. My mistake, as I could not but notice the two guys who suddenly appeared on either side. I thought to myself, those two are twins, as I caught a glimpse of them. Both were as gorgeous as the bartender, dressed in black tuxedos, white shirts unbuttoned, and tanned skin glowing. I found myself sandwiched on three sides. No, wait. Their hands moved swiftly to my rear, cupping my buttocks with their soft, sensual hands. They touched down in unison, then squeezed and did not want to let go. With gentle firmness, I felt their touch against the red of my dress. I held my breath and glanced at my watch. Only two minutes had passed.

CHAPTER TWO

I clenched my backside, reacting to their touch. My pulse was suddenly racing. I could smell the musky heat that these two strangers were giving off. The heady aroma of their closeness made my head spin in a daze of desire.

The hot bartender, having made my drink, reappeared in front of me. Tanned, with a hint of shadow that men who choose not to shave every day for the edge it gives them, he was staring right at me with his piercing blue eyes glimmering beneath a full mop of hair that fell on all sides. I like the effect of longer hair in men. His disarming smile made me gush. He placed my drink in front of me and thrust a bar cloth deep inside a glass he picked that did not need cleaning. But he wanted me to watch him toying with the glass. In a way, I wished he were doing the same to me right now. My momentary distraction allowed the other two to pull up a couple of bar stools and wedge me firmly between them. I had no escape. And escape was the last thing on my mind at that moment.

Their arms shifted in unison as they took me underarms and swept me off my feet, easing me onto the barstool they had positioned behind me. And there I was, perched on high, a captive in a triangle of art-deco barstools. Now they could justifiably turn toward me. Their legs spread wide as they positioned themselves to either side, willing me to do the same. My knees quivered slightly. I could do nothing but give in to the temptation to follow suit, easing my legs apart slowly, just enough so that my legs touched theirs. And all this time, my handsome bartender kept up the pretence of drying the glass in his hand, his eyes unwilling to release mine from his penetrating gaze. Still, no words came out. No casual lines to make me smile. Just the simmering look of handsome men filled with desire – an erotic craving for me.

I held my breath, the anticipation of what might come next causing me to fear I would soon need to touch myself. The throbbing need grew more intense with every passing moment. And in the blink of an eye, they moved again. Their timing was impressive. With the gentlest of touches, their hands reached out and fell softly on my knees. Then, for a moment, their passage upwards along my thighs began, unwavering, intent, until they reached the pinnacle of my hold-ups. The lace tops were a barrier between where they had come from and where they intended to go. I watched as they continued their journey, taking in the luxurious sight of them climbing the heights of my aching thighs.

I feared they might turn back as they paused at the lace confines of my stockings. But, after resting there for moments to take in the view, they pushed on, over the edge, under my dress, and into the darkness beyond. Their touch was no longer shielded from my soft skin by protective nylon defences. They made first contact with my suspenders and then with my skin.

For all I had tried, my inner thighs were moist from the excitement. I turned to all three of them, in turn, as the moment came when my two guardians reached the final obstacle to their goal. My by now soaking wet underwear. Little more than a feeble defence to their approach.

The softest of touches from their fingertips told me they had arrived. The pressure applied to the meagre patch of material, all that stood between them and my hungry sex. I could feel the desire in their eyes, all the more from them sensing my heat. They toyed with me, pressing their advantage until I could resist no more. Then, I leant forwards with a rush of what I can only imagine was the closest I had ever come to an instantaneous orgasm.

Such was the suddenness of the moment that I stretched both hands in front to avoid falling into the bar. But my hands did not rest against the bar. Instead, unconsciously, they went for the nearest firm holding they could find. And I found myself clutching onto their stiffening cocks, hidden out of sight but not out of mind. I looked down in shock, and another wave took me, my legs now weak from desire. I could not resist the desire to look at where I had landed, my face full of surprise. And I noticed my watch, the dial glowing in the semi-darkness. Another two minutes had passed by.

CHAPTER THREE

The feel for art-deco had always appealed to my lover and me. Something about the look made everything we did together a little decadent – as if we had travelled back in time. That is why he – my lover, my escort in all things of this kind – took such pleasure in hunting out items of lingerie and jewellery that reflected those bygone days. We both took pleasure from the sense of luxury that came from looking refined. And, for tonight, we had chosen a vintage-look suspender belt and a diamond choker as part of my attire.

The metal clasps of the suspender belt pressed hard against my thighs. Seated as I was on high, they gave a little extra pleasure-pain as I soaked up the attention of the two men beside me. In the background, music from yesteryear played softly, compounding the sense that one might have of finding oneself altogether in another, better time and place.

As I have gone to such great lengths to describe my wardrobe that evening, I might as well add a little more. What little else I wore beneath my red jacket dress was designed to thrill whoever might be so fortunate as to garner my favour. Whilst all around the crowded room seemed oblivious to my situation, the three men closest to me gave me their full attention. I was slowly getting heady with desire.

Whilst this might not have been the first time I had been the centre of more than one man's attention, having witnesses to such evident and consenting misbehaviour was a first for me. I looked down, taking in the sight of two handsome men's hands caressing me intimately. Their fingers were well-versed in how to excite a woman. From gentle caresses to deep delights, they weaved their magic touch along and between my legs.

I confess to being mesmerised by their touch. So much so that I did not notice when the bartender moved away. Looking up, I felt a momentary wave of disappointment. Was he the one out of the three I lusted for the most? The two men, hands tightening firmly on my thighs, brought me back into the moment, and the smile returned to my lips. And, as far as the bartender is concerned, I need not have worried, as the evening for me had only just begun.

Finally, though in truth only minutes had passed, the conversation began. I admit it was more a series of compliments from the two of them on my appearance, perfume, and dress. In particular, the jewellery around my neck aroused their interest. The choice to wear it had been a good one.

As we spoke, I caught them looking at each other. Just a momentary glance. But immediately, their hands slid gently away from where they had been resting against my warm thighs. My hands remained firmly in place, one on each of them, holding them nice and tight.

I only found out how they did it later, but at that moment, all I remember was them gently taking my hands in theirs, forcing me to surrender my grip on them. I did not want to let go, but needs must, and I enjoyed giving in to whatever they had planned for me.

For an instant, I thought that their gesture was a romantic one, taking me by the hand. That was until they brought my hands forward and still holding me, laid them to rest on the bar's edge. The distance from the barstool to the bar was precise, and I found myself leaning at almost 45 degrees. What were they doing?

Someone reaching across from behind me gave me a clue. Holding a glass of champagne, the mystery arm stretched past me, depositing the drink on the bar, directly in front of me, between my firmly planted hands. I recognised the rolled-up shirt sleeve and the musky smell of his skin. It was my favourite bartender. He had vanished just a minute or so before and reappeared behind me.

I started to turn my head to see, but a firm squeeze of my hands from the two men told me not to do so. At the angle I was at, all I could do was move ever so slightly to my left or right, meeting the gaze of one or other of them. The bartender, if indeed it was him, was off-limits to my eyes.

Neither the champagne on the bar nor his hands against my waist were off-limits. He positioned his hands where my waistline descended toward my thighs. The curves of my body were accentuated by his hands clasped firmly against me.

Both men released their hold on my hands, allowing me to decide for myself what to do next. I remained still for moments, luxuriating in the feel of this sexy guy's hands squeezing me tight as I observed the champagne flute in front of me.

It served its purpose almost immediately when his hands grasped my jacket dress at the sides and pulled it upwards in a slow, deliberate motion. It was a short enough dress for me to know that he would discover what kind of lingerie I was wearing beneath in seconds. I grabbed the champagne and took it down in one breathless gulp.

As I had imagined, no sooner had I returned the drink to the bar than I felt his touch on my naked derriere. With my dress offering scant protection against his advances, he had the pleasure of being the first to discover my choice of underwear for the evening – a backless number I had received as a gift from my lover just days earlier.

Something in my mind flickered – a momentary thought that came and went instantly. But enough of an idea to make me smile again. Did my lover know what was coming? Did he plan this? The thought excited me even more.

The champagne I had consumed hit my sweet spot. Suddenly, all my timidness disappeared, and in its place came an uncontrollable urge. I wanted all three of them together. With my newfound freedom of movement, I took my hands off the bar and returned them to where they had been. I landed perfectly on the stiff outlines of their cocks to either side of me. And, instead of straightening myself upright, I leant forward further, offering the bartender the best view in the house.

His hands tightened on my naked cheeks, caressing them with enthusiastic abandon. Then, with the same abandon, he leant his body against mine. His breath now close to my neck, he stroked my skin as he journeyed from one side to the other. Then I saw his face as he leaned forward to kiss my lips. I turned towards him as best I could move my head, still caught as I was between the two suitors, and our lips met. We kissed passionately as I clenched those two hard cocks in my hands while he squeezed my butt cheeks hard. I was now oblivious to everyone else in the room.

After what seemed like an eternity, our lips parted, his kiss filling me with a craving for more. I looked down, the sight of the other two excited bodies I held onto simply adding to the pleasure. I glanced at my wristwatch. Four more minutes had passed.

CHAPTER FOUR

The bartender brushed his face against my hair, speaking softly. A table had been prepared for us, and I was momentarily taken aback. Why was he interrupting this moment? His hands released their hold, my jacket fell back into place, and as suddenly as he had appeared, he vanished into the fray.

My two partners wasted no time standing to either side of me, forcing me to release my hold on them, but not before looking at what I was letting go of. Too much temptation was slipping out of my grasp as the seconds passed. This was not going the way I'd expected!

They offered their outstretched hands, gesturing me to step down from my seat. I reluctantly followed their bidding, landing on my high heels as they once more took my arms. Moments later, they guided me away from the bar, an empty cocktail glass the only reminder of those heated minutes of lustful play. And still, that internal voice was telling me that there was more to come.

We made our way through the crowd of strangers, who, despite being engaged in their private conversations, were warming to each other's attention. I noticed this for the first time since I'd arrived. It was far more intimate than one might expect in a public place. Hands were caressing, necks were being subjected to passionate kisses, and the scent of desire filled the air like a powerful aphrodisiac.

Something else I noticed was how, whilst the men were exclusively attentive to their companions, the women all seemed to turn towards me as I passed by. Then, like waves rippling as you glide through the water, the calm returned as I swept by on the arms of my two gentlemen.

We reached our table. It was tucked away in the corner of the room, with its leather rounded seating to provide the perfect viewing point. The table was perfectly positioned to people-watch, hidden from view if I wanted something more intimate, away from prying eyes. There was no doubt as to which direction I wanted us to take.

I slid onto the luscious leather seating, my two guardian angels, as I had hoped, taking up position on either side of me. We tucked our legs neatly under the long white tablecloth that could hide a multitude of sins. There was no possibility of any misbehaviour being caught by passers-by. I felt a renewed sense of anticipation. And what happened next caught me completely off guard.

The bartender arrived with a silver platter balanced perfectly on one hand. I watched as he glided skilfully through the madding crowd. His body arched one way, then the other as he avoided contact and maintained our drinks in perfect equilibrium. I didn't immediately notice the stunning brunette following him until he reached our table and stepped to one side. Her presence was unmistakably purposeful. I watched, transfixed, unable to avoid staring at her. Dressed in a figure-hugging, sequined black dress, she looked dressed to kill. Her lips were a deep ruby red, and her eyes never left mine for a moment.

She waited, unmoving, as the bartender took each drink in turn from his platter, still held high, taking his time to position each one precisely in front of the three of us. Then he lowered his arm, bringing the tray directly to the girl. There was a momentary pause. That instant before something unexpected happens.

The girl reached for what seemed like an empty tray, too high for me to see, and picked up something hidden from my view. She had deftly picked up two silk, black ribbons, and something else before I could make it out.

At that precise moment, my wrists were once more captives of the two men. Their hold this time was more secure, more dominating. I realised I had been holding my breath and let out a gasp before taking in an even deeper lungful of air. Where was this going?

The girl wasted no time in leaning, full-bodied, across the table. Her dress did little to hide her pert breasts from view. I was in the front row of her performance. Her lips and curves gave me much more than a little bi-curious emotion. My wrists, now held in front of me, offered no resistance as she took the silk ribbons and tied them neatly, ensuring they were tight enough to give me no hope of escape. With my wrists firmly bound, my guardians loosened their grip on me. With the bindings now secured, she pulled them toward herself. My body leapt forward, my breasts planted on the table, and my head could do no more than look ahead, fixed on her lustful gaze and swollen nipples. She leaned toward me until her lips brushed mine, her breath falling hot upon me. And still, she held the ribbons tight.

Just then, I heard something coming from both the left and the right sides. I sensed what the sound was but could not be absolutely sure. I was unable to see, held willingly hostage by my female companion.

Moments later, her grip on the ribbons loosened. She straightened up and offered a ribbon each to my two companions. Having released their hold on me earlier, they took the ribbons and pulled gently, easing my wrists off the table and to the sides. My hands fell onto their legs as they continued to draw them down. But I dared not take my eyes off the woman. Her look of desire was burning into me, and I did not want to let go.

If I needed confirmation of the earlier sounds, I got it as my hands came to rest upon their stiff cocks, now freed from any form of clothing. They stood waiting impatiently for my attention. I grasped them firmly, one in each hand, feeling them throb with delight. The girth beneath my fingers made me want to take a closer look.

I gave in to temptation and broke off from the woman's intimate gaze, admiring what I now held in both hands. They were deliciously attractive cocks. Perfectly formed and sufficiently excited to make me feel pangs of hunger. I wondered whether I should lean over to sample their delight or if it was best to let them lead. As much as they wanted to be in control, they were enjoying the attention they were getting. They were throbbing to my touch, and as I squeezed, their response came straight back. Both of them arched their bodies ever so slightly. Finally, the first sign of weakness!

Then, as suddenly as I had seized control, they wrenched it back, and their free hands took a firm hold on my knees. We all paused for a silent moment of complete physical contact. Then I felt that familiar gentle pressure as they began to ease my legs apart. I looked at them in turn with a look of bemusement, curiosity, and pleasure. What were they planning now? I turned to the bartender, standing in front of me with an expression I can only describe as satisfaction on his face. He was enjoying the show. I then turned toward his female companion. At least, I intended to do so, but she was no longer standing there. In those few instants of distraction, I had not noticed her move away. Where has she gone so quickly? I looked into the crowd beyond, but she had vanished.

My legs came to a halt, not too wide to be uncomfortable, but just enough for me to feel slightly exposed. Luckily, the tablecloth hung well, hiding my less than the ladylike position from general view. And then the penny dropped. I realised where the woman had gone as soft feminine hands slid between my inner thighs, pushing my legs further apart, and I felt her warm breath once more on my lips, but this time, down there. I gasped again and could do nothing to stop thrusting my thighs forward as her tongue dived deep into me with no warning. Both my hands tightened as I held on for dear life. I glanced at the watch on the bartender's wrist. My time was up, but I couldn't stop.

THE UNICORN

*Is having your first bi-curious meeting an easy thing to do?
It appears to be anything easy when you are a woman who
wants a woman looking for a woman like you. So, when
you do, make sure it's something very special for you.*

FLASH FICTION ONE

Through the open door, the room was inviting, with a wonderfully large bed taking centre stage. Hazy sunlight through half-drawn curtains bathed everything in a twilight glow. Bedside lamps merely added to the sense of warmth already filling the room. We entered, our coats on, bags in hand, leaving behind the daylight, retreating from reality.

A sense of nervous anticipation filled us both, our thoughts spinning with the weight of a thousand emotions. We closed the door behind us, our bags placed carefully down, coats removed and hung carefully away, all in total silence. And once we had completed the ritualistic motions, we swiftly closed the space between us, our bodies together, arms around each other, eyes meeting eyes, lips touching lips. Our kisses were passionate as ever. And yet, today was different somehow. Days and weeks passed as we waited for this moment to arrive until we finally arrived. The wait was over. The time had come.

We began the day with that which all lovers do, embracing each other in a slow, steady crescendo of foreplay mixed with conversation, anticipation, and then lovemaking. Our bodies were connected physically, and our thoughts united as one. The curves of our bodies were aligned in perfect unison, one with the other. And still, we waited, even while we made love.

While we took pleasure from each other's bodies, we counted the seconds passing by, slower now than ever. Time, though silently passing, took us forwards until, in perfect unison, we were close to the point where love overflows into climax. Then, as if rehearsed to perfection, a knock came at the door.

We fell silent. That often fantasised, never realised moment had finally arrived. She looked at me and smiled a nervous smile. Her hand reached out to gather black lace from the floor, the lace hiding her nakedness from view. Her lips touched mine.

She walked silently toward the door, her hair still dishevelled from our lovemaking, skin glowing from the warmth we had created together. She reached for the handle, resting it there. After a long pause and a deep breath, she opened the door to meet the woman of her dreams...

RED LETTER DAY

Sometimes, the unexpected can be more exciting than the things you plan. And when they happen, the thrill they bring can take you to places you never imagined.

CHAPTER ONE

Looking out of the floor-to-ceiling windows of the beautiful third-floor rented apartment, we held hands. We watched the sun sink slowly beyond the horizon. The warmth of a long summer day gave way to red skies and early evening shadows. Today was the twelfth day of the seventh month of the year. My birthday had come around once more. But unlike any previous birthday, this was going to be unique. A day when my desires were to become a reality. A party with friends, mostly with benefits.

We had planned this day for a long time, selecting those we should invite and discussing what we might want to do. But we fell silent on the topic with little more than a month to go. It seemed to have been forgotten. Perhaps it was too much to expect fantasy to become a reality. At least, that's what I thought until the evening of my birthday. We had settled on dinner at an up-market restaurant. I arrived at our rendezvous and was surprised he was not waiting for me. It was only when the limousine pulled up beside me. The tall, dark driver stepped out and opened the rear door for me, and I realised the evening wasn't going to go exactly how I thought it would. He was good-looking too!

Laid out on the back seat was a very sexy dress, accompanied by high heels, expensive lingerie, a Venetian embroidered mask in red and black velvet, what seemed like a blindfold, a bottle of equally expensive perfume, and a handwritten note. Dark chocolate truffles, champagne and flutes completed the ensemble. The door closed behind me softly, soft sensual music filled the air, and the wheels began to turn as I settled into my seat. I opened the note with nervous anticipation. It was his handwriting – a series of instructions to be followed to the letter. This was unexpected. My pulse began to race.

"My darling," the note began. "Happy birthday, and may all your wishes come true…" I knew from how he wrote that those dots meant he had more planned than the phrase implied. It continued, "Your driver has been instructed to stop three times on your journey to me. You must not get out until you've reached your destination. You will know when you've arrived. For now, all you need to know is that you should change into the outfit prepared for you at your first stop. At the second stop, your driver will blindfold you. Do not worry; I will be keeping a watchful eye on you."

Well, that was mysterious. What was he planning? And what did he mean he would keep an eye on me? I put the note down and looked out of the window. Where was I being taken?

No more than a minute later, the limousine pulled in and parked. I tried to work out where we were, but I'd gotten disoriented and didn't recognise the area. The darkened glass that divided the driver seats from the rest of the car slid down with a quiet hum. His voice was the sexy kind of deep that made me shiver. "I have been asked to wait here until you have changed your wardrobe," he said. "Please tap on the glass when you are done." And with that, the dividing glass closed again, hiding him from view.

With so much space in the back, I quickly slipped out of my attire and into my new outfit. I was a little hesitant at first, having to disrobe completely. Still, my mind was already drifting onto how well-toned the driver was, and that voice was enough to melt away any residual shyness I might have had, replaced by a slight longing in my thighs.

Everything fitted perfectly, the lingerie was clearly of the highest quality, and I could check my reflection in the smoked glass. I looked simply divine. The dress, of course, was to die for. Deep red, short enough to make every head turn, and deep enough at the front to hold me vicariously. He knew my taste in clothing too well.

I tapped gently on the diving glass. The engine roared into motion once more. I sat down, adjusting myself, and the car eased into the evening traffic onto my next destination.

CHAPTER TWO

The city's bright lights slowly awakened as the sun dipped below the horizon, its final hold on the day just past now, giving way to the first shadows of the night. The limousine was my only companion as we drove towards the next stop. And then we were there.

The smoked glass divide opened again, and through it, held tight in leather gloves, another envelope was passed my way. Again, not a word was spoken. I leant forward, took the envelope, and the divide closed on me once more. This time, the instructions were straight to the point, "Move to the centre of the seat. Slide your dress up to the hems of your stockings. Place the blindfold around your eyes and rest your hands by your side." No more than that, and I gladly chose to obey.

A moment passed, and then some more, and nothing moved. The car stood still. I waited, listening, expecting, I don't know what. Until the only sound to be heard was my beating heart. And then a sound. An echo too? Or was it both the doors unlocking? Then the cool evening breeze brushed against my skin, and the car rocked. Finally, the sound of someone entering. But without the gift of sight, just sound, I strained to sense which side it was. Maybe it came from both sides at once?

The doors closed in unison, but this time there was no mistake. I heard their closing sounds an instant apart. Two had opened, two had entered, and two had closed the doors. My breathing deepened as the seats beside me shifted with their weight.

Whoever they were, there were two of them, and they were on either side of me.

The engine roared into life once more, the music took centre stage, the volume raised enough to mask the sounds of life outside, and the darkness deepened by my lack of sight. And then, they touched my thighs.

Whoever they were, they moved in unison. Warm hands – thank you, gentlemen – caressed my legs, slowly moving from my knees to the boundary of my lace-top stockings. Gently, sensually, and without urgency. My body tingled with excitement. I had never been blindfolded before, let alone finding myself in a car with strangers. Yet, the fact that he was behind this was all the reassurance I needed. And, he had said in his first note that he would be watching over me. Perhaps he was one of them?

I knew I wasn't meant to peek, but I wanted to. Who were these two men? Would I like them if I saw them? But the blindfold was thick and wide enough to make sure I wouldn't be able to sneak a glimpse. And then their lips caressed my neck. Two men kissed me, sending shivers down my spine. As instructed, my hands were by my sides, and now I knew why. I could feel their legs against my fingers, their bodies now leaning into me. And my fingers had a mind of their own.

I understood why he'd chosen a limousine. The seat was deep and wide, and the musky scent of leather added to the sensual atmosphere. One glass of champagne had already affected my senses, freeing me from any residual inhibitions there might have been. I knew what he wanted from me. My complete surrender to his desires and my own. Warm, soft caresses of expert touches on my skin were doing the rest. I felt my dampness growing, adding to the cocktail of aromas filling the air.

Still blindfolded, my hands moved of their own volition, climbing onto willing thighs seated to either side of me. In the darkness, I moved to find their growing desires, sliding my hands in unison along their legs until my sense of touch told me I had arrived. They were both impressive to the touch. I held on tight, gentle movements urging them to respond to my touch. And respond they did, growing in excitement at my eagerness. Their throbbing filled me with a sense of urgency, and my dampness became a torrent.

The car continued on its journey, and we seemed to have all the time in the world. Enthusiastic kisses, first from one, then the other. Their bodies came ever closer to mine, and their strong, powerful arms envelop me, leaning into my body in a delicious crush. My hands worked hard to release them from their clothes, their hands working beneath the fabric of my dress, the lace of my underwear. And they continued to move as one, with purpose, on my legs, on my breasts. Then they descended together until their fingers touched the edges of my panties. I felt myself losing control, my pussy throbbing with desire. And then they were in. Sliding their fingers beneath the lace, tugging my legs apart, and easing apart the lips of my sex with their expert touch.

I wanted them inside. I needed to push my body closer, using their fingers to give myself some relief from the sexual tension building inside me. And they worked their magic. Softly, gently at first, building up slowly, taking me with them as I held on tight to their now hard cocks.

I pushed harder against their touch, wanting to make myself

come. They responded in kind, deeper inside me with urgency now. And I was now a torrent of damp desire. Taking their now naked cocks I held on tight as they took me together with their touch. The blindfold just added to the intensity of my other senses. I felt every movement, heard every groan, and tasted their lips against mine. And then my mind clouded, the rush of a powerful orgasm taking over. I gripped them harder, tugging at them both in a desperate attempt to bring them with me. It was working. Their moans grew louder, and I knew I had to hold on to my self-control a little longer until they were ready to release themselves under my spell.

And then we came. Together. At once, cream on my hands, and I let go. The waves went on and on for what seemed like forever. I had never done anything like that before and lay soaked from what they had done to me. Finally, giving in to the moment, I loosened my grip, and they followed suit. And we rested together, exhausted by the journey taken together.

One last scene remained, still keeping to the script. They took cum-soaked fingers to my lips, inviting me to lick them clean. They tasted delicious, so I improvised, taking their cocks, and drinking them dry. And then, we all smiled before our tender goodbye.

DOWN THE STAIRS

How do you know when you can give yourself completely to someone? By putting yourself in their hands? Trusting them to do whatever they want with you? If you really want to find out, try wearing a blindfold. It's a good place to start.

FLASH FICTION TWO

A guiding hand led me, step by step, down the stairs to the dimly lit basement, my high heels echoing on wooden staircase treads. The utmost attention to detail kept me from the merest of glimpses of my surroundings. A blindfold and mask were my companions on this journey into the unknown.

My lover was by my side. As I descended slowly, I recalled his words spoken just moments earlier.

"I will be your guide, and I will be your eyes."

Once the stairwell gave way to firm flooring, I knew we had arrived at our destination. My vision blurred, other senses attuned to the sounds and scents surrounding me. The smell of lustful bodies filled the air, becoming more noticeable as I penetrated deeper into this place, my lover's hand still safely holding mine. The sounds were unmistakable. Sighs and moans from lovemaking; some of those sounds were slow and sensual, others wilder, more urgent. And another sound, that of flesh against flesh as bodies entwined in erotic desire. There were sounds to my left and right, all around.

I knew my lover had exquisite taste. He would ensure I had nothing but the best. Even so, the lack of sight made me nervous. I wasn't clear whether it was anticipation, hesitation, or both gripping me, but every second felt like an hour. My breathing was shallow; my skin was damp from the body heat of those around me.

"Now, kneel." came his command.

I felt the collar around my neck pulling me toward the ground as my lover took the lead and made me obey. My knees bent in response. His hand assisted my descent until I touched the floor and found myself in total subservience. He was in command. I was in his hands.

He let go of me. The lead in his hand was now pulling so that I had to lean forwards. My reflex was to raise my hands in front of me, unable to see where he was taking me.

At that moment, I first felt them, right in front of me, at the same height as my face. What one lacked in girth was made up for in length. The other had both in abundance. I held on to avoid falling and found myself gripping both cocks firmly. I squeezed them both as if to confirm what I already knew them to be. Stiff and throbbing, there before my very eyes, though I could not see.

I held on as my lover brought my face closer until I could see in my minds-eye that I was within reach. My lips widened as I made first contact, widening as they drew me in until I took the nearer of the two in my mouth.

The leash fell loose. My lover's hand was now behind my head, taking my hair in his grasp. Then with slow, purposeful motions, he pushed then pulled my head forwards and backwards, repeatedly. My lips tightened on my prize, sucking, then releasing in rhythm. Now firmly in control, my hand followed the same motion as I patiently worked this stranger in my mouth.

After ten or so strokes, my head was shifted to the other man, held firmly in my other hand. I let my lover's hand guide me in a steady motion, first with one, then the other, slowly making me build the pace and force of my actions.

Though I could not see the effect I was having on them both; I could feel their reactions in my hands and on my lips. Their breathing grew to a crescendo as my lover skilfully directed me to ensure their passions rose in unison.

Then, the hold on my head shifted, keeping me firm between these two men. My hands pulled together, their cocks taking centre stage, just in time to take a direct hit as they released over me, engulfing me. My mouth tried to stem the flow. And still, they continued until they could come no more.

I released my grip on them slowly and deliberately while I savoured every drop. This was going to be a night like no other, and it had just begun.

THE GAMES PEOPLE PLAY

What do two couples do when they lock the door behind them? Are most people strait-laced, or do they go further? And what does further really mean? How do four people, all of whom have their own individual desires, find a mutually pleasurable balance? How do they bring their fantasies together under one duvet cover?

CHAPTER ONE

Summer is my favourite time of year. Warm sunshine, long days, balmy nights. And on those rare days when the summer lives up to its name, I enjoy staying up late in the garden or at a rooftop cocktail bar, where the cooling breeze brings some respite to a hot, intense day of lounging in the sun. This brings me to my story.

It was precisely on one of those occasional hot days, a Bank Holiday to boot, where your body is damp with sweat as you sunbathe, sunglasses perfectly positioned, bikini fitted, smartphone in hand to swipe aimlessly from topic to topic. My sun-lounger was strategically positioned to keep an eye on any attractive strangers passing by when I came across a face online that I hadn't seen since an office party back in the noughties. She'd moved away shortly after that first unforgettable incident.

Since the reawakening of my sexual desires, they had gone into overdrive, and I had become insatiable in my appetite for naughtiness. No point in having a day off just because the sun was shining. And suddenly, at the sight of that face, I once knew, I felt an unexpected wave of lust deep between my thighs. Could it be her? I had to find out.

Twenty minutes of internet searching later, I was convinced it must be Toni. She'd matured in looks but remained delectable. She was my only experience of sexual impropriety with another woman – though back then, I think we both classified ourselves as taken but stirred.

We'd known each other for years, when the evening of the office party, for no specific reason, Toni called me over to join her for drinks with the latest in a long line of boyfriends; David, as I recall. To cut a long story short, the evening began with drinks and laughter, only to develop into a deep dive into all of our sexual fantasies – few, to be honest. David had been pushing her to try a threesome with two girls. She pointed him out to me, flirting in a dark corner with a couple of the office staff. He was good-looking, enough for me to pay more attention to his body than what he was doing, so when I got invited back to his place with Toni for a nightcap, I was happy to tag along.

Fifteen minutes later and we found ourselves playing spin-the-bottle on his bed. It wasn't long until I discovered just how racy Toni was. Her tongue found the ideal playground between my legs, and David's cock was big enough to make us both hungry to taste it. I'm sure I came a couple of times as Toni knew precisely what she was doing, and David was more than happy to take us in turns. We finished late into the night with a glass of cheap plonk and our faces covered in his warm, salty cum.

CHAPTER TWO

So, fast forward a dozen or so years, and here was Toni's face staring back at me from my smartphone. The memories of that night came flooding back, and talking of flooding, I had to change my bikini shortly afterwards as my fingers had taken it upon themselves to play with my damp, throbbing pussy, while I had been reminiscing about that night.

After a little more digging, I found her Facebook page. Minutes later I posted a message, assuming she would remember me. After all, certain things are unforgettable!

I didn't have to wait long. She came back with a long rambling note on how she'd missed me so much, and we had to meet and catch up with our backstories. She was living in London with another in a long line of used and abused boyfriends. I didn't ask whether she had ever married or not. It seemed a little irrelevant.

After exchanging messages, she kicked into her old-fashioned flirty banter, asking what I'd been "up to" and if I was having "fun." She seemed to be the same old Toni I had known and enjoyed hanging out with back in the day.

With such fantastic weather set to last into the weekend, we wrapped up with an agreement to meet up that Friday for drinks in London, with friends in tow, of course.

Getting through the week was a pain. Looking forward to one event or another just seemed to make the days drag by. Luckily, I'd had the chance to break up the monotony of the week with a couple of dates with Zach, one of which ended up with us popping another little cherry on the bonnet of my car. And I'd had it valeted the week before. My butt cheeks felt all tingly between the feel of the hot metal and his equally hot rod. I think we managed to avoid being seen by the passers-by!

Zach was equally excited at the prospect of meeting the one and only woman I had ever had sex with. However, I told him that he was to be on his best behaviour and that naughtiness was entirely out of the question – much to his disappointment. Still, he managed to tease out of me a series of confessions about what I'd done that night and how often I'd done it. He said he was jealous of David. I told him to grow up and wait his turn.

Finally, Friday arrived. We caught the early train and checked ourselves into a hotel a short distance from where I'd arranged to meet with Toni. The usual big bag contained our change of clothes for the evening and an assortment of toys, old and new. We weren't going to miss the opportunity of having a little fun ourselves once we'd wrapped up the date with Toni plus one.

CHAPTER THREE

Come the allotted time, I had slipped into a short black and gold party dress with my new heels – a present from Zach. He took his time to clean up beautifully in something akin to a tuxedo, just toned down enough to look delicious but not over the top. We were ready. I grabbed my clutch and his hand, and we headed to the agreed meeting point.

You can imagine the shock on my face when we all met at 8 pm. Toni's plus one was none other than David. They both looked great; my first thought was of his fantastic cock. I had to pinch myself to refocus on social niceties. I gave Toni a bemused look as if to say, "weren't you with some other guy?" but her look of complicity kept me quiet. She'd done this on purpose, the sneaky madam.

David, of course, took the opportunity to give me a knowing hug, much to my embarrassment, as Zach looked at us, trying to assess the situation. I remained silent.

We spent a pleasant couple of hours at a delightful bar in central London, keeping with the usual parameters of those who are meeting for the first time in a long time. The cocktails were delicious, and I suspect that Zach and David were plying Toni and me with doubles whilst they kept to singles. By ten o'clock, my head was spinning, and my pussy wasn't far behind. Here I was, in trendy London, surrounded by three people I'd had the most pleasurable sex of my life, and we were doing our best to be polite and well-behaved. I shouldn't have worried. That was all about to change.

At ten o'clock on the dot, David looked at his expensive watch and said, "Right, let's go somewhere more fun." Toni glanced my way, and I saw a glint in her eyes that I remembered well from our fun times together. She grabbed her things and stood up. "Come on, you two," she said, "let's see what the night has to offer."

We stepped out into what was left of the summer heat onto the crowded walkway. People were having fun inside and outside the various pubs, bars and restaurants that filled the streets. We walked on, not daring to ask where we were headed, but my chest was tight with the sixth sense of the evening being far from over. I wasn't wrong. David and Toni had an agenda as we arrived at the doors of a well-known gentleman's club. Two hefty bouncers vetted everyone as they queued for entry. We breezed through with a knowing nod from one of the bouncers. David and Toni were well known to them. Interesting!

CHAPTER FOUR

Passing through the doors of the club was like entering another universe. Bathed in dim, red lighting, with dark, sumptuous furnishings throughout, the inside looked like something from a magazine for hedonistic interior design. I knew Zach would love every moment, as he'd tried on more than one occasion to invite me into such a club, but I'd always resisted.

Thick leather seating filled the place, with a long, art-deco bar and matching stools covering all one side of the room. Small, booth-like rooms spread around the remaining walls, giving the whole place a sense of erotic intimacy.

Then, there were the girls. Although there were a fair number of customers, it seemed like an equal number of young women were working there. From the bar staff to the dancers, they swept around the place knowingly, sensual hunters looking to make eye contact with you. They were all dressed in the most provocatively tasteful way, giving you food for thought as they stopped to say hello and see if you were interested in a private dance in one of their booths, hidden far from prying eyes. We passed on their advances for the first hour, limiting ourselves to enjoying the stage acts as they came and disrobed to the sound of music designed to arouse even the saintliest souls.

Things started to heat up at the point that Toni and I decided to go to the bathroom together. We were already well-oiled and had fits of laughter in the toilet as we exchanged lusty comments about David and Zach. We agreed vocally that both were utterly fuckable. We also managed to cram our latest sexual leanings into a discussion that lasted no more than five minutes. Toni had decided to up the ante on her sexual activities over the past couple of years, having been married to someone – not David – for the better part of twenty years with no more than a dozen sexual relations during that time. Finally, at the tender age of fifty-five, she decided there was more to life and walked out. The rest, as she said, was history, but she was having the time of her life. We agreed to continue the conversation later.

Back at the table, David and Zach had wasted no time being accosted by a lovely lady sitting between the two of them with one leg over each of theirs, giving them both a stunning view of what might be. Toni and I walked up and managed to look both annoyed and approving at the same time.

Toni took the initiative and sat beside Zach, giving me no option but to do the same, this time next to David. Boy, he smelled good. Whatever aftershave he used was seeping straight down between my legs. I had to find out what it was and then give Zach a bath in it.

Toni piped up, "Are you boys getting what you want?" That mischievous glint in her eyes again as she laid her hand on Zach's leg, just high enough to make his cock throb with unexpected anticipation. I looked at Zach and saw his approving eyes undressing me as Toni touched him. I wanted to see what happened but got distracted as I momentarily looked down and saw the size of David's cock, hard in his trousers. God, he didn't just smell good; he looked good too. Any resistance was futile. Making sure Zach and Toni could see what I was doing, I leaned back and moved my hand slowly enough to make everyone in the room pause, down, down, lower down until it landed gently but decisively onto his bulging manhood. His response was immediate and positive.

Toni took the opportunity to stand up, lean forward and whisper in the young woman's ear. She nodded, acknowledging the request, and brushed herself past us, leaving the four of us again alone. Toni had managed in a single movement to dispatch the girl, and to leave her sexy backside, barely covered by her red party dress, inches away from Zach's lustful gaze. For my part, I got to see her perfectly shaped breasts and just a hint of nipple as she leaned forward. I noticed for the first time that evening that my panties were soaking wet.

Needless to say, the rest of the evening went well. Luckily, we were all seated together with a table in front of us, hiding our misdemeanours from the rest of the public, give or take the sideways glances thrown our way by curious by-passers. By midnight I had wrestled David's cock out of his pants and was enjoying a slow stroking session. He knew what he was doing too. His fingers craftily worked their way beneath my dress, past the last defence of my crotchless panties, and neatly into my crutch, making my wet knickers even more soaked. I swear I almost came twice. All of this whilst making ever increasingly racy conversation.

Zach was enjoying the show that David and I were putting on, whilst Toni was busying herself with a remote-control toy that she had slipped inside herself a little earlier. Not once did she let go of Zach's cock, now undoubtedly aching to be taken to completion. Toni's gentle moans of satisfaction just added to his – and our – excitement. And yes, she came at least once.

CHAPTER FIVE

By one o'clock, we were all on the edge of reason. This time, Toni came to the rescue, suggesting we retire to somewhere cosier. I seconded her idea, my vagina screaming silently for more than a playful fingering. I wanted something nice, big, and stiff inside of me.

We grabbed our things, leaving a sizeable tip for the girl who had served us drinks for the night and kept Zach and David occupied. Then we headed into the night. This time the temperature outside had fallen quite noticeably, and I shivered as we stepped onto the street. Zach wrapped himself around me to keep me warm. He pointed in the general direction of our hotel, and we headed off together, walking as four people who've had a couple of drinks do. David spent the majority of time with one hand firmly on Toni's backside. The other hand was on mine. Halfway to our hotel, we had a pit stop whilst Zach helped Toni remove her remote-control toy– with his teeth! I kissed him straight afterwards. I wanted to see if I could taste Toni on his lips.

Although our room was on the third floor, the journey took several minutes – we just kept pressing different floor buttons. Alcoholic confusion. In any case, except for two occasions when other hotel guests gate-crashed our lift party, I managed to French kiss first one of them, then another, then the other. I counted three different kisses, or four. Maybe one of the hotel guests got more than they bargained for when they took the lift. Anyway, we eventually got out on the third floor and made our way to the deliciously spacious hotel room. Zach always did like to splash out when we went to London.

Now, to say I didn't see this coming is an understatement. By this time, I was sure we would tear each other's clothes off and end up in a seething mass of bodies on the super king-size bed. How mistaken I was. Toni was way ahead of me in her world experience. I had a great deal of catching up to do.

With the door firmly locked behind us, David and Toni made a beeline for the desk in the corner of the room. David's hands went straight to the television cables as Toni dipped into her bag. Moments later, they connected a DVD player to the television. Zach and I watched motionlessly. I swear both our mouths remained open in astonishment. David turned the tv on, and the DVD stirred into life. A quick play with the remote control and the screen burst into life. High-class porn streaming directly onto our screen. Toni seemed pleased and kissed David on the cheek before pulling a large bottle of Prosecco out of her bag, followed by four crystal glasses. Someone had been planning for this eventuality. Sneaky madam.

Zach and I exchanged glances, and he gave a slight shrug of his shoulders. I took this to mean, let's just see what happens. He took my hand as we stood side by side at the door.

David slipped off his jacket, showing off his magnificent body in white shirt and trousers. Toni had already disrobed, exposing her deliciously dangerous curves in a figure-hugging dress. Moments later, David popped the cork with Toni holding onto the two wine glasses as he filled them to the brim. She turned and proffered them to us before returning to fill the remaining two vessels. Then we stood together, glasses in hand, the sound of groaning bodies filling the room as the video played. They smiled at us. Two playfully mischievous smiles. As we sipped the

Prosecco, Toni said, "Let's play."

"David," she began, "loves to watch me play with others. He's kinky that way." I shot a look at David, who had seated himself comfortably on the bed, facing us, and the television. His shoes and socks had somehow come off in those few seconds, and he was busy gripping that big cock of his through his trousers, squeezing it gently to warm it up. I just wanted to take it and feel him filling me up, but it looked like I'd have to be patient.

"Now then," she continued, "let's see what we've got here." With that, she dived into my bag. I'd let slip that we'd brought a few toys along, and she was quick to latch onto that thought. She pulled out the black bag of goodies, unzipped it, and emptied the contents onto the bed. "Mmm," she murmured as her fingers scattered the toys left and right. Then her fingers stopped on something I'd not seen before. Another of Zach's new toys he'd bought for the occasion. A neatly wrapped length of red rope. "What's this?" she asked. "Who was going to tie who up tonight, then?"

The way she spoke and moved was making me hot with anticipation. I had flashbacks to her tongue between my legs all those years ago. She was good then; imagine what she might be like now. I forgot about David's cock for a moment as my eyes soaked her up. She had the most delicious ass. I thought about running my tongue between her butt cheeks, all the way around until I could taste her again.

She picked the rope up and slowly began unwinding it, moving towards Zach as she did so. I watched as if I were watching a movie. The sound from the DVD playing added to the sexual tension that was growing by the second.

She walked past me, handing me one end of the rope. "Hold this," she said and continued toward Zach. "I think we are going to have fun with you tonight," she said to Zach. "Aren't we, Isa?"

I shook myself mentally and decided to get into the game. "Absolutely," I replied.

CHAPTER SIX

Zach stood his ground as we approached from either side. Then, in unison, Toni and I slipped Zach's jacket off and unbuttoned his shirt, fingers toying with his chest as we did so. My fingernails cut into him as I ran them down his front, reddening his skin. Toni took one of his wrists and tied the rope around it, nice and tight. Then, she fed it through a clothes hook against the wall and yanked it, causing his arm to rise above his head as she tethered him to the hook. A knot to hold it tight left him almost hanging there. "Don't move," she murmured. Then turning to me, she said, "And you, don't let go of the rope." I didn't remember her being so dominant, but I was enjoying it.

She turned her back to me before ordering me to unzip her dress, which I did dutifully. The sound of the zipper opening was by itself a turn-on. Her naked back was now exposed as she turned toward me. "My turn," she said before making me turn around, allowing her to unzip my dress which she did so deftly before slipping the dress from my shoulders and letting it fall gracefully to the floor.

I stood there in my best deep scarlet underwear. An expensive matching brief and bra set, with suspender belt and stockings adding to the effect of sumptuous luxury, complemented by high heels and perfume to match. I felt the gentlest of touches as she ran her fingers along my neck and down the back of my body. My whole being shivered with pleasure. She turned me around to face her. As I turned, I caught the first glimpse of David's massive cock, now freed from all restraint, succumbing to his gentle massage. His eyes were firmly locked on my body, his growing excitement all down to Toni and me.

Now facing Toni again, I returned her lustful gaze as she slipped the dress from her shoulders, allowing it to slide slowly downward, exposing her breath-taking figure in the tightest corsets I had ever seen. Her waist was half the size of the rest of her body. Her plump, round breasts heaving to escape their prison, her sex glistening with damp arousal. She wore no knickers.

Then we kissed. I will never forget the feeling of another woman's lips on mine. The gentleness was a stark contrast to masculine kisses. Then, we discovered each other's tongues once more. The first time in a long time. I ached inside. I wanted this. We embraced. More than just a momentary closeness, this felt like more. I enjoyed her arms around me, mine around her. Our bodies squeezed into the tightest of spaces, with all eyes upon us. It felt like a dance.

And then, it was over. We released each other and took a step back. The smile on her face told me that the night had just begun.

"Now then, Zach," she started. "What are we going to do with this delicious body of yours?"

"Isabella, what do you think? Should we make the most of this rope?"

"What did you have in mind?" I asked.

"Let's see," she replied. "Let's get these clothes off to start with."

We began to undress Zach slowly and meticulously, starting with his shoes and socks. He'd been less prepared for this than David. That was a first! Then, Toni unbuckled his belt and undid his trousers, pausing long enough to run her hand over his growing manhood. She leaned in to kiss him as I watched. My man was being manhandled by this woman. I loved it.

"Help me with these," she ventured, referring to his trousers. Together we eased them down and off, leaving him in his unbuttoned white shirt and dark, figure-hugging underwear. Something was fighting to get out. Another pass of her hand on his stiffening cock, and the movement below was undeniable. His free hand grabbed my shoulder as he reacted to her touch.

"Time to make use of the rope," she whispered. "Wrap it tight around his body."

I did as she commanded, tightening the rope with each pass. Zach was enjoying the experience. Around his chest, around his waist, and then two passes around his thighs. He looked cute in red.

"Is that tight enough for you?" I asked, joining in with the conversation for the first time.

"Mmm, yes," was all Zach could muster in response. His eyes flit between Toni and me, with the occasional glance at David – or his cock. I was beginning to enjoy myself with this little game.

"Now then," continued Toni. "Let's see what you've got to offer the ladies." We looked at each other with an understanding that had proven over time. Then, we kneeled in front of him. Each of us took a corner of his underwear and, teasingly slowly, tugged downwards, biding our time until the moment his stiff cock finally emerged in a magnificent show of pure lust. We gazed at it, two hungry creatures, ready to feast on him.

"Wait," said Toni. She stood once more, facing Zach, her lips inches away from his. Her delicious mound was now just inches away from my lips. The temptation to taste her was almost overwhelming. But I was curious to see what else she was up to.

She ran her long fingernails along Zach's chest, scarring him gently. Then, as if by second nature to her, she grabbed his free wrist, yanked it upwards and looped the rope around it, tightening it as she went, leaving him now completely powerless, both hands bound.

"Mmm," she purred. "Now we've got you where we want you," she said. She licked his face as if to show him who was in command.

"Let's eat," she said, looking at me with a greedy glint in her eyes.

We feasted on Zach's cock and balls for ten minutes, teasing it to grow. I watched as Toni slid him shamelessly into her mouth, forcing herself to gag on him as she swallowed as much as she could. Then she took me by the hair and pushed me onto him, forcing me to take as much as she had done. I gagged as the length of his cock burrowed into my mouth.

Then she kissed me. A kiss that I remembered from the past. Instants became hours as I delighted in her exploration of my mouth. Her hands were around my face pulling me in with passion and desire. Zach's cock hung loose as we shared our feminine pulsations in front of these two gorgeous men.

David, meantime, had disrobed completely. To say he was fit would be an understatement. He was very fit. And very well endowed. I couldn't stop myself from the occasional look of unfettered want in his direction. He seemed to reciprocate, purring in a manly fashion at the show unfolding before his very eyes.

"First, we do one. Then we do the other. And then we do each other." Toni's directions were clear. How she wanted us to act upon them wasn't. But, by this stage, I was more than happy to go with the flow.

CHAPTER SEVEN

I wasn't the only one who had brought along a goody bag. Whilst we had returned our attention to Zach, with Toni milking his cock with long, luxurious strokes, feeding the tip of his cock into my mouth, urging him on, she turned to David and said something I didn't catch. It didn't take me long to understand. I discovered that Toni had become something of an expert in many areas. David reached over to Toni's bag and rustled around for a moment before pulling out toys that, individually, would have made me raise my eyebrows. But all together? What was she planning?

David passed across what looked like two silver, weighted balls with a long piece of black twine hanging from them, a large bottle of what could have been oil or lube, and two pairs of long satin gloves. My mind when into overdrive, imagining what she intended with them. Her steamy glint had turned to pure lust mixed with playful pleasure. I looked like she was enjoying this more because of the look on my face and the undoubted pleasure she gave me.

Taking the twine, she carefully wrapped it around Zach's balls. Tight enough to make him wince, not too tight to hurt. She continued, weaving her magic around the length of his cock, making sure the sensitive tip was free to breathe. The weighted balls did the rest. Hanging from the end of his cock, they provided enough leverage to heave it downwards, causing the kind of pressure that keeps a man hard for a long time. Sneaky Toni. She wanted Zach to remain as hard as he was for a while yet.

Opening the bottle, she poured it onto his stomach at just the right point for it to ooze downwards and along the length of his shaft, covering it is a sleek patina of oil. It glistened in the light, a delicious, wet stick of rock waiting to be eaten. The fragrance of the oil was familiar.

"Edible," was all she said. I don't know whether she meant the oil, Zach's cock, or both.

"Now, Zach, let's get you a little more comfortable, and don't you dare let that gorgeous thing go down on us. You can keep playing with it, but don't even think about coming."

I found her dominance quite exciting. I began to wonder when my turn would come.

Toni unhooked Zach from his hanging place and pulled him toward the empty chair in the corner of the room. He followed without a word, keeping his eyes on me all the time, with a cheeky look in his eyes. I could tell he loved this too.

Once seated, Toni released Zach from his bonds, except for the weighted twine that continued to exert a pull on his cock. It showed no signs of deflating. If anything, he was getting a little harder still. It was hard to tell at this angle.

"Your turn," she said, meaning me.

By now, my panties were soaking wet, and my whole essence was throbbing with need. I could see two splendid cocks begging to be consumed, yet here I was, just following orders. I yearned to try them both. I didn't have to wait long.

Toni took my hand and helped me stand. I stayed silent, wishing to be the best I could be for her. I wanted her too. I wanted her to make me come. Just her and me.

She pushed me onto the bed and lay beside me. On the one side, David. On the other side, Toni. Déjà vu. If Zach was a tasty seven inches of pure delight, David was just as much, if not a little more, and equally good to look at too. Their fingers began to explore my body. It was as if they intended to take me back to the place it had all started – and ended after one encounter – with them, way back when. I closed my eyes and took it all in. The ambience, the sensations, the lust seeping through my very being.

As I lay there, enjoying the attention, I glanced across at Zach. He was devouring the scene with a look of pure delight. His cock, thinking that now was not the time to suffer from stage fright, remained strictly to attention.

Toni kneeled in front of me and, in one elegant movement, carried one leg across my body so she was now over me, her wet pussy hovering over my face. Oh god. I knew exactly what she was about to do and what she wanted. I stared, unblinking, as she lowered herself until she was a hairbreadth away from my mouth. Instinctively, my tongue emerged and approached her. With the tip of my tongue, I finally tasted her sweet nectar. Delicious. I suddenly realised how hungry I was for her, and my hands grasped her waist as I pulled her onto my face, emerging my mouth with her moistness. I buried my tongue deep inside, and she gave out a moan for the first time that evening. She was enjoying this, and that turned me on even more.

I felt David's hands around my ankles. Whilst I had been distracted with Toni, he had taken the opportunity to run his tongue and fingers between my legs. Such had been the pleasure of tasting Toni that I had hardly noticed David's attentions. But now my mind came into focus, and I finally took in the joy of having sex with these two again.

My ankle slowly rose into the air as David handed them off to Toni. She took them with a firm grasp. Her ability to multitask was impressive as she raised and lowered herself onto my face to get the most out of my attentive tongue. Now my feet were firmly in the air, spread apart as far as Toni's outstretched arms would reach. I was wide open to David's attention and didn't have to wait long.

CHAPTER EIGHT

Since meeting Zach, I've had the pleasure of playing with several men – always alongside him – but I hadn't experienced a man as well-endowed as David. The tip of his cock pushed firmly against my pussy, but I should have expected this from these two by now; he held it there for an unbelievably long time. There was enough pressure for me to want the next inch but not enough to suck him in. And in the position they'd gotten me into, I could not move an inch in any direction. They were making me wait. Toni continued her up-down movements, and I could feel her edging towards something special. Then they moved in on me together in the blink of an eye.

I felt the first drops of Toni's gushing run between her thighs. Her breathing was deeper now, her panting becoming louder. The taste of her honey began to fill me as she exploded into my mouth. A wet gush ran down my face as she yanked my legs back and shook with delight at the orgasm I was giving her.

David took that as his cue. My swollen wet sex was no match for his stiff, eager cock. He thrust it deep into me, making my eyes open wide as I felt the rush of his shaft drilling deep inside me. With my legs airward, held tight by Toni, I was in no position to resist. I gasped. Then, again and again, he took me deeply, unwavering in his effort to fill me. The suffocated groans coming from me now just spurred him on. And Zach sat motionless, taking in the sight of his lover being pounded by this man. His cock twitched excitedly.

Toni and David were kissing each other as one attempted to drown me in her love juices, and the other was doing his best to bring me to orgasm. I had to let go. This was too much pleasure for me to resist, and they're right to say resistance is futile. Giving in is much more fun.

I came in wave after wave of pure pleasure. My body quivered as he continued to thrust, paying attention to my contractions and timing them to perfection. Then slowly he relented, slowing to a grinding halt, his thick meaty cock buried in my body.

Toni arched herself off me, allowing me to breathe again. She lay exhausted by my side, gently stroking my hair and kissing me. David collapsed onto me. His fit, muscular torso crushed me with intense delight. I had just been pleasured by these two for only the second time in my life, and it was simply amazing.

Toni smiled at me and then stood up. Her powers of recovery were impressive. Then, as I lay there with David by my side, she moved in for the finale.

"A little birdy told me in the toilets that someone here likes anal sex," she broadcast mischievously to her audience. She looked Zach in the eyes.

"Good, I see you enjoyed the support act. Now for the main event."

She leant forward over Zach, her peachy buttocks smiling at me, and gently undid the twine holding Zach's cock in place. Then, reaching across, she picked up the two pairs of satin gloves and threw them to one side. "These," she said, "are for later."

She stroked Zach's cock, the oil spreading evenly across his shaft. Then taking a little more oil, she bathed her two middle fingers in it and slid them gently into her backside. David and I took in the view, his fingers stroking his cock once more.

I watched, eyes wide open again, as Toni turned to face us, her back now to Zach, still firmly seated, standing to attention. She spread her legs to either side of Zach's legs and passed one hand between her legs, grasping his cock tightly. Then, ever so slowly, she eased his cock into her backside. I watched as it vanished inside. This was going to be a long night.

LET ME WATCH YOU

*When your lover enjoys watching you with others,
what do you do? You say yes, of course.*

CHAPTER ONE

I had never been watched before. I didn't consider it an option. It wasn't something I'd ever thought about. But then, I always got a thrill out of being slightly submissive, guided along the way. But to excite me, the guiding had to lead down some dark, unanticipated path. So, when I was instructed to wear a short, classy number as we were going to an up-market bar in the city, I did so without hesitation. Expensive jewellery, divine perfume and extremely high black heels completed the look. I felt fabulous and with way too little covering way too much of my body. Still, I enjoyed the attention I would undoubtedly get.

We arrived a little after 9:30 pm, late for us, but we'd arranged well in advance that we would stay over at the Hilton just down the road from where we found ourselves. The place was already buzzing, and we had to work through the crowd to reach the bar. My partner leaned over to one of the bar staff, who pointed to some unoccupied seats across the room. We ordered drinks and then headed to our reservation. A corner niche with velvet seating and a drinks table. Smoothly done. He did take care of the finer details. We sat down in our preferred "people-watching" position and made a toast. His hand made a beeline for my well-exposed thigh, resting there with a gentle squeeze. I was glad he had made an extra special effort to dress up in a delightful tuxedo that fitted in nicely with the rest of the crowd. Very swish indeed.

We chatted for the better part of half an hour until our drinks had been downed, and it was time for a refill. We usually took turns and having confirmed I wanted another Pinot with soda water, he headed for the now three-deep bar. I took the opportunity to study the local fauna more attentively. The women were stunning, and four out of ten men were pretty nice too. Not a bad return for a Friday night, or any night for that matter. My gaze drifted from one person to another and then to the next, mentally scoring each out of ten. My attention was elsewhere when a stranger approached and sat beside me without asking. I jerked as I was about to tell him the seat was taken when he reached into his inside jacket pocket and pulled out a red envelope. My heart skipped a beat.

My gaze flipped from the envelope to him and back again. I registered an eight out of ten for his looks somewhere in my mind. Why was I thinking that? But I knew that a red envelope could only mean one thing. Someone sitting next to me for the past thirty minutes had arranged this. I looked up towards the bar, but there were too many people for me to make him out. So where had he disappeared to?

I took the envelope and opened it, still flicking my eyes between it and the man sitting beside me. I read the message it contained slowly and deliberately. Then I reread it. One sentence, four words: "Let me watch you," was all it said.

I took a deep breath and returned the note to the envelope, closing it and placing it in my handbag. I needed a cigarette right now, and I don't smoke! Only then did I notice that this stranger had brought me a drink. Yes, of course, it was a Pinot Grigio with soda water. I uttered my first words to him, thanking him for the drink. Then, his hand made a beeline for my well-exposed thigh, resting there with a gentle squeeze. Deja bloody Vu!

We began talking, though in a most erotic fashion from the

outset. He told me his name, clearly already knowing mine. He also told me he had been given incredibly detailed instructions on turning me on and that I was to allow him the opportunity to do so. A few kisses on my neck and lips told me he had paid attention to those instructions. His roaming hand on my thigh helped convince me further. And whilst he took to his task with warm abandon, I looked across the room from time to time to see where you know who had gone. I guessed he had hidden where I couldn't see him, but he could see me. That's what he'd set out to do.

CHAPTER TWO

With the place so crowded, nobody could see as my new neighbour slowly slid his hand beneath my dress, which by this time had risen of its own volition way above my knees, exposing my thighs to anyone who cared to glance down as they came by. His fingers were weaving their magic between my legs, and my body responded eagerly to his touch. The thought that we were being watched suddenly became exciting as I thought about how turned on someone would be watching me enjoy myself. I took another sip of my wine, deciding it was my turn to let my fingers do the walking. I bravely lowered my hand onto his lap. What awaited me was... concerning? My god was he already hard! Without thinking, I squeezed my fingers around it, and although his trousers did an excellent job of protecting him, I think I may have gasped out loud as I could barely reach around his cock. I felt slightly anxious, compensated by more than a hint of dampness between my legs. I sure as heck hoped someone was watching us right now.

I shifted position once more, both hands now free to do what I now felt the uncontrollable need to do. I unzipped his trousers with a single swift movement and thrust one hand inside. God, he was commando too. His stiff cock almost sprang out to meet me, and I made contact. I wrapped my fingers around my prize, barely managing to hold on. One final pull and out it came in all its magnificent splendour. My eyes opened wide as my brain tried to do the calculations. It was longer and thicker than anything I'd seen up close before. I didn't even think I could stretch my mouth that wide. But I wanted to try. I wanted to give my hidden admirer something to make him hard too, and maybe even wish he were sitting right next to me now to get a better view.

I took a moment to look around, making sure nobody was watching. Honestly, a couple of guys were doing so discreetly, but they were both seven out of ten, so that was fine, and if they wanted to, there were two empty seats beside us.

My head disappeared below table level as my lips homed in on his swollen manhood. I made first contact, pausing before doing my best to engulf him. I lowered my head slowly as he stretched me with every passing inch. I made it to five inches before I retreated momentarily. That was nice. I repeated the same motion several times as I put hours of study into practice, gently squeezing his balls with one hand as I held onto him with my other hand, applying just enough pressure to make him throb. He tasted delicious, and I lost track of time, only stopping when my mouth began to ache. I looked up at him and caught him transfixed on me, with what I can only describe as a very sexy glint in his eyes. I finally lifted my head above the parapet. I kissed him on the lips, my tongue burying itself inside his mouth, making sure he savoured the taste of his cock in my mouth.

I looked around again, and, for sure, those two guys were enjoying the show, their cocks rigidly to attention as they tried to behave as if nothing was going on. I was tempted to wink at them but thought better, as they may have taken it as an invitation to join in. Maybe later?

CHAPTER THREE

The place was now heaving, and goodness only knows if my watchful companion was enjoying the show I was putting on. Still, I was going to give him the performance of a lifetime. I sat straight and slid both hands beneath my dress. This was going to be fun. Then, keeping my eyes on my companion next to me, I eased my sodden black undies down my legs. I slowly slipped first one foot, then the other out, holding what resembled a wet cloth in my hand. I raised it to his face and let him smell how hungry I was for him. Then, without any consideration for the crowd, oblivious as most of them were to what had just happened, I threw one leg over him and straddled his thighs, facing away from him.

To any unknowing onlooker, it just looked like I was sitting on his knees as we both looked at the crowds in the bar. To the very few who knew instead, you could see what I was doing from the expression on my face. I took hold of his cock between my spread-wide legs and shifted position, so the tip was poised on my lips. Then, releasing my grip, I eased myself ever so slightly down, halting myself as he now made first contact with me. I felt myself stretch and gasped once more. Then, looking across the room, I finally found where my other man was sitting. He had the perfect view of what I was about to do, and the look on his face told me everything I needed to know. He loved me and loved what I was doing.

Leaning forwards so my hands sat flat on the table in front of me, I lowered myself inch by inch onto his massive cock. I held my breath as he entered me for the first time, my body adjusting to his size. I kept going until I thought it could go no further. I couldn't feel his thighs against mine. Just how much more did he have to give?

As sure as night follows day, my rising and falling gathered pace. As it did, I felt him going a little deeper each time until the flesh of our thighs finally made contact, and I felt his abundance consume me.

I continued the same steady movement, up and down. His hands were firmly on my butt cheeks, assisting me with the exercise. And slowly, our breathing became shorter, our pulses faster, until I felt him arching slightly backwards. I had been ready to let go for a few minutes, but I'd held out, waiting for him to catch up. And here we were, the two of us, ready for our finale.

I clenched myself as hard as possible, tightening my grip on his massive cock. I thumped down on his thighs, harder each time, willing him to explode inside me until he finally did just that. I felt a stream of cum shoot deep inside, his cock like a fire hose, filling me with warm, salty pride. I screamed silently at the orgasm I'd been gifted from this guy.

Finally, it was over, and I leaned forward on the table, speared on his now softening cock, his cum leaking, covering us where we were firmly joined at the hip.

I didn't move until his balloon had fully deflated. Even so, he was of sufficient size to remain in place, so I decided to ease myself up and off. The insides of my legs were wet with his cum, as was his cock. I figured it was a shame to let it all go to waste, so I leaned in and savoured some dessert. He tasted divine.

We embraced once more, adjusted ourselves, and he kissed my hand before taking his leave. I found myself alone once more, with just a few knowing eyes looking my way. It was time for my man to return. Again, I looked his way, a twinkle in both our eyes. He stood up from where he'd been sitting all this time, adjusted his arousal and headed my way. But, before he could reach me, two guys who'd been enjoying the show decided to come and say hello. They made themselves comfortable before he was halfway, so I looked up at him and smiled a knowing smile. I'm sure I told you they were seven out of ten, didn't I?

NEW YEARS EVE

Cosplay is another one of those things that people do – dressing up in costume for Halloween is a good example. Perhaps you've dressed up on New Year's Eve to attend a Fancy Dress party? Maybe the event was a little racier? With all the superheroes now on our screens to choose from, which one would you choose? I know who I would want to be. Miaow!

CHAPTER ONE

From October through March, the nights last long enough to give the night meaning. Busy streets are brightly illuminated, whilst the quieter parts of the city bathe in a weaker but still endearing glow. Every house is ablaze with light, though hidden by curtains drawn. The mood of quiet slumber embraces the world once the sun disappears beyond a distant horizon.

Gone are the long lazy summer evening, sitting outside, socialising with friends and acquaintances. To be indoors whilst the sun still shines would be a guilty sin. Now, as Winter fast approaches, we can once again afford ourselves all the guilty sins we desire, hidden as we are, behind closed doors.

New Year brings with it the mandatory social festivities, and this year, with my lover in hand, it took on a whole new dimension. Patiently, over several months, we had built up a circle of, let's call them intimate friends. A dozen or so kindred spirits, all eager to make the most of life and love. And so, we talked, planned, and plotted until everyone had agreed on a theme for our year-end party – superheroes.

Naturally, this wasn't going to be any old superhero party. Absolutely not! Imagine the fun to be had in finding the most outrageously sexy costumes, both for the group's men and women. We banded together to undertake our research and ensure we agreed on who would wear what. We compared our finds from Superguy to Batguy and Wonderful Woman to Cat Lady and collectively made our purchases online. We banded together to rent an apartment in the city centre for the night. Then all we had to do was wait. The scene was set, and the location was too. All that remained was waiting for the party to start.

We'd arranged to meet at a local venue, having purchased tickets for the fancy dress event. That way, we would easily fit in with the rest of the crowd, albeit with far racier costumes than everyone else, but hey, we didn't care as we all wore masks.

The evening panned out nicely at the bar, with everyone having a wonderful time and flirting outrageously. It wasn't just between us that fun was being had by eleven o'clock, as several good-looking guys eyeing us up had been invited to join our group. We adjusted their costumes to make them fit in more with ours. That involved a lot of strategic ripping off clothing. However, they didn't seem to mind.

We were determined to remain until the New Year had been welcomed in. A little after midnight, I lost count after numerous French kissing sessions with everyone in our extended group, both men and women alike. I'm sure there were even a couple of strangers who just happened to be standing near me and got in on the action.

CHAPTER TWO

To cut a long story short, my Cat Lady outfit was the outright winner that night. I got my claws into several guys, and more than one got their fingers into me. I especially enjoyed clawing the Guy of Steel, who lived up to his name, if you know what I mean.

By the time we got back to the apartment, the group had grown to around twenty guys and girls, quite a few a little worse for wear with all the drink that had been flowing. Somehow, we all managed to squeeze into the lift – a maximum capacity of ten people. That was fun. I'm not sure who was behind me, but I wanted his number later, that was for sure. We tumbled out of the lift and, a few moments later, locked the apartment door behind us. That's when the party started.

During the next few hours, I learnt a lot of things I'd never known before. For example, when Wonderful Woman decided to sit on my face as I lay on the floor, I discovered that it was pretty hard to breathe. Luckily, my cat claws came in useful as I slid two of them into her backside whenever I wanted her to lift herself a little. It also helped my cause that she was busy eating a guy dressed like the Incredible Hunk. I had a perfect view from below of his cock being swallowed whole by Wonderful Woman as she gyrated in my mouth. Watching her technique, I made mental notes along the way. I especially noticed how she leant forward to create a straight line from her mouth to her neck. That's how she managed to take all of him with consummate ease. And that little trick of stroking the tip of his cock with her index finger.

Noted for future reference.

I was distracted for a moment by the sound of Superguy and Batguy, the latter being my lover - at least, I think so, as we'd had a couple of other Batguy lookalikes join us. They were busying themselves with Superlady on the sofa. She was riding Superguy, who lay still on the couch – perhaps he'd passed out – while Batguy was busy attacking her from the rear. She was making enough noise to wake the neighbours. Luckily, Spiderguy took the initiative to fill her mouth with his cock, muffling her moans.

Back on the floor, some unknown partygoer had spotted that I was pinned down by the weight of Wonderful Woman, still grinding her groin into my face. I was unable to resist his advances. I felt my legs lifted skyward and knew exactly what fate awaited me. My thighs followed, being raised by powerful arms. This could only be one man – the Black Tiger. My pussy quivered with nervous tension as I'd already felt what damage he could do earlier at the party when I was on a clawing rampage. His tongue ran between my legs, but it was hard to tell if he'd made a difference as wet as I was. But when he pushed his tongue deep into me, I realised it wasn't just his cock that was impressive. I calculated it must have been at least three inches long. I could hardly wait for the main course.

The Incredible Hunk struggled to resist the continued deep throating he was receiving care from my female companion. His body shook with a wave of pleasure before he collapsed to his knees, his balls hanging above my forehead, his cock mere inches from my lips.

Thankfully, in shifting his position, he forced Wonderful Woman to adjust hers too, and she finally slid down from my face, allowing me to join her in performing oral sex on the Hunk. In turn, she took his cock and fed it to me before removing it from my mouth and sliding it into her mouth once more. At one point, we ran our tongues together along the whole, delicious length as he came closer and closer to surrender.

As I took him in my mouth once more - this time determined not to be outperformed by Wonderful Woman and simultaneously resisting my tendency to gag on large objects, I realised the Black Tiger's tongue had vanished. In its place was, oh my god, his big, bad cock! It slipped into me like a freight train entering a tunnel, only this tunnel was only just wide enough to take it. I buckled with the pleasure-pain as he entered me at high speed.

Now I had superheroes coming at me from both ends. While I enjoyed the sublime feeling of being filled by them to the brim, the penny suddenly dropped as to what both men were doing. I bet they'd rehearsed it beforehand. They were taking Wonderful Woman and me at the same time. She'd sneakily eased her bottom downwards until Black Tiger had the two of us at his mercy. And he was making the most of it, thrusting first into one, then the other. Similarly, the Hunk was enjoying the attention we were giving him, in turn, and together. For some reason, men just love to have two tongues on their cock, at the same time!

What seemed like mere moments later, although it was probably more like ten minutes, our two super guys reached their peak together while we ladies were still on an upward arousal curve. Oh, well, better early than never! I felt an explosion of creamy cum hit me between the legs, filling me up, at the same time as the Hunk released himself all over my face. Miaow! I think they'd both been saving their strength for a few days as they continued to shoot all over me for countless seconds. And when they finished, Wonderful Woman descended onto my face, eager to clean up the mess left by the Hunk, after which she collapsed onto me, and we concluded our battle with a long, lingering kiss.

I had to admit, this was one heck of a New Year's Eve party, and the fun had only just begun.

WAKING UP IN PARADISE

Have you ever woken up after a night on the tiles, remembering little, if anything, of what went on? Even worse if it happens on your first night on holiday with your lover. If it happened to you, would you be shocked to discover that you were capable of a lot more than you had ever imagined? The most important thing is to be sure that your lover loves you just the way you are – and maybe, just maybe, if you are as bad as you can be, he will love you even more.

CHAPTER ONE

Have you ever dreamt of waking up to the sound of waves lapping up on a nearby beach? The bedroom blinds shifted gently and silently, ebbing and flowing in time to the rhythmic movement of the late summer breeze. That was my experience the morning after the night before. What a night!

I lay there unmoving, my face submerged in the fragrant softness of a fluffy white pillow. My hair felt like a thousand hands had run wildly through it, giving me the look of a satisfied woman. I raised my head gingerly. I was unsure whether a sudden movement would hammer home the message that there were consequences to consuming – though I prefer the word savouring – cocktails the whole night through. I should have known better at my age, but, after all, the things I'd done last night were things I'd waited a long time to do. I had no regrets at all.

The fog lifted slowly from my mind. First, my arm shifted from beneath my pillow, falling to the side. Then, lying as still as possible, without hazarding to turn my head, I fumbled with my free hand until I located the warm, naked flesh of a man's torso beside me – either that or it was a very toned woman. Either way, I'd had a result last night.

My fingers did their best to identify my neighbour. Was it my boyfriend, Zach? I ran through the catalogue of men's torsos I had explored in the previous twelve hours. Luca, maybe? Or Tom, perhaps? No. This body had a different feel to it. Who else could it be? My mind slowly cleared as I pieced together the previous night's events. I felt pretty confident those were the only men I had the pleasure of meeting, or maybe not. What about the two guys whose names I didn't catch? Had they wandered off after Luca did his thing to me? I really should have stopped at three cocktails!

I resigned myself to accepting whoever fate had landed in my bed, turning slowly towards the sleeping beauty beside me. And there he was, peacefully asleep, my tasty Mediterranean boyfriend, Zach, with a woman's black lace bra over his head! And for the record, it was not one of mine!

I lifted my head and did a quick scan of the room. There was no one else in sight. My brain waking up now, I checked underneath the bedsheets. No extra legs or arms there. I then switched to listening mode. With no unexpected sounds coming from the bathroom, I felt relieved. It appeared that there were just the two of us in the room, so I couldn't have behaved as badly as I thought. Still, whose bra was that anyway, and how did it end up on his head?

CHAPTER TWO

Zach stirred from his slumber, opened his big brown eyes and greeted me with a big smile. My pussy reacted instantly. He had that effect on me. I savoured his first luxurious kiss of the day, long enough to please me, brief enough to tease me. He wished me good morning before leaning over to one side and showing me his stiffy. Well, hello to you too, big boy! Whether it was morning glory or simply that he was pleased to see me, I really didn't care. This was day two of our long-awaited holiday, and I was going to get as much of him as I could squeeze.

Before that, though, I had to find out who the owner of the bra was. So, I reached over and picked it off him. I shifted into slow motion. My movements made sure the mystery woman's garment rubbed against his skin. I dragged it into his line of sight, swiftly applying a fake look of annoyance to my face. I intended to play the jealousy card just for fun.

He looked at it indifferently. Men have no idea what cup size means unless they have their hands all over it. He looked at the bra, then me, then back to the bra. Nothing. No raised eyebrows or blushing cheeks. None of the typical guilty male behaviour of immediately playing things down or finding an excuse for the unjustifiable. I started to wonder if he was innocent of all charges. Instead, he simply shrugged and said it must have belonged to Jade. Who the heck was Jade? Oh, right, now I remembered. Another new face we met on our first night. I needed to moderate my intake. My memories of her and the two guys she was with came back to mind.

So, the next question was, how did Jade's bra end up on his head, in our bed, in the morning? I looked at him with my best prosecution lawyer face, ready to cross-examine the defendant. Then, just as I was about to begin my questioning, a groan came from beside the bed.

I clambered over Zach like a lioness hunting her prey and peered over the cliff edge of the bed. There on the floor lay a pile of tangled bodies. They were, I now recalled, the owner of the bra with two guys she'd been playing with on the sofa last night. Well, that was the bra mystery solved. But what about the two guys? What were their names? I paused to think. Luca, of course – mmm, nice body – and the other? Her partner, maybe? Tim? Tom? Maybe not? A thought crossed my mind, and I rolled back across the bed and checked the other side. No, there were no more naked bodies hidden in plain sight. So that made five of us in the room. Cool!

By this point, I had forgotten about Zach's morning glory, waiting to be put to use. On the other hand, Jade seemed interested in what she saw as she raised herself onto her knees beside the bed and was presented with a front-row view of Zach's naked butt. "Well, good morning to you", she purred before sinking her teeth into his bottom.

Sweet innocent Zach did what all well-behaved men did in such circumstances and yelped. He then rolled over to respond to Jade's greeting, giving her another rousing view. Unfortunately, my reaction was just too slow, as his cock pointed straight at Jade's face, her eyes popping wide open and her mouth doing the same. What a way to wake up! I had to nip this in the bud before my man got more than he expected from the woman kneeling beside him, naked as the day she was born, sporting quite impressive boobs, I have to admit.

"Time for a cuppa," I yelled, throwing the bedsheet over Zach, doing my best to hide his arousal. I leapt out of bed and grabbed his shirt, which had been thrown casually over a chair. Wrapping myself in it, I made my way to the coffee machine, skipping to avoid stepping on the bodies piled on the floor. I noted that both were well-endowed as I hopped over them.

I greeted them with a "Good morning, gentlemen, time to get up."

As they stirred and opened their eyes, my naked butt crossing the horizon was the first thing they said. That got a collective moan of approval. This had the potential to be a very interesting breakfast.

"And who, might I ask, are you two?" I inquired innocently as I readied the kettle, standing beside them. I gave them a panoramic view of my legs, to their evident delight, as they both rose rapidly to the occasion.

"Who, us?" one of them replied. Still half asleep and suffering from the same malaise as the rest of us, now with a cheeky grin on his face.

"Claudio. And my friend here is Lorenzo."

"Ciao, bella", responded Claudio. He had a sexy accent. They both did.

"You both Italian?" I asked.

"Si", came their response together. The image of a sticker with the words "two for the price of one" somehow popped into my head.

"Buon giorno ragazzi", I replied in the sexiest voice I could summon, using up what little Italian I knew. These two were definitely worthy of my attention later on.

The roomful of bodies began to stir from their resting places like zombies rising from the grave. They queued to use the bathroom and proceeded to cover themselves as best they could. It looked like much of what they must have been wearing the night had been lost along the way. I had no recollection at what stage of the evening proceedings we had all moved to our room. I'd ask Zach later, but from the look on his face, he seemed as oblivious as I was to the events leading up to them being there.

Given that it was an all-expenses paid holiday, we ordered room service, figuring the hotel wouldn't complain about us ordering five of everything. A short while later, our buffet breakfast arrived. Remembering the cute staff member, Luca, I moved before anyone else, opening the door wearing Zach's white shirt and nothing else and with the buttons still undone. Oops! Sadly, it wasn't him. I did my best to hide the look of disappointment on my face. I had been turned on at the thought of opening the door to one Luca Di Silva - room service par excellence. When we arrived, he'd shown us to our room, and I'd made a mental note of his name. Oh, well, I'm sure I'd get another opportunity to flash him.

Having brought the food and in, the five of us sat on the bed and had our first menage with croissants, orange juice and copious amounts of tea and coffee. How Italians can drink so many espresso shots first thing in the morning is beyond me. I'd be stuck to the ceiling with all that caffeine. At this point, all thoughts of ardour had subsided, and everyone decided to retreat to their rooms, freshen up and begin the day anew.

Zach and I cleared things up and made the best of adjusting the bedsheets before falling back onto the bed for one more kiss and cuddle. Only then did I ask what had gone on the previous night. He looked at me and shrugged his shoulders. I could tell he was as much in the dark as I was. I'd just have to ask around later on that day. At least we knew three other people who might fill in the gaps.

CHAPTER THREE

Having freshened up and dressed appropriately for a day of rest and relaxation, we wandered down to the beach and set about doing as little as we could for as long as possible. My sunglasses offered my poor throbbing head a little respite. On the other hand, Zach seemed to take everything we had done – and consumed – in his stride. I did like the fact that he was younger than me. My toy-boy.

That said, I had to admit that my new friends, Luca, Claudio, and Lorenzo, were all pretty young compared to Zach and me. I guessed that Luca was probably in his mid-thirties. On the other hand, Claudio and Lorenzo had the air of forty-something playboys – single, footloose, and fancy-free, with a dress sense to turn a girl's head. They seemed inseparable – a dream team. Or was it a tag team? Well, either way, this was the sexiest group of people I'd met in a long time.

Lying on my all-expenses-paid sun lounger, I felt a tingling sensation between my legs. I lifted my head and tilted my sunglasses up. There it was – the tell-tale damp patch on my otherwise perfect bikini bottoms. I was getting the tiniest bit turned on with my mindful dalliances. Why was I getting so frisky? Oh, wait a minute. Could it be the perfectly toned, tanned men lying naked all around me this morning? I had so much temptation before me and so little time to act.

Thankfully, my phone alert brought me back to my senses. I shook off the warm, tingling sensation and sat up, legs spread across the two sides of the sunbed. My sun hat offered a degree of respite from the searing sun. Zach lay next to me, arms behind his head, soaking up the warmth, his flat stomach leaving me in little doubt that I'd chosen wisely. I was a lucky lady, greedy for his presence.

My phone alerted me once more, and I picked it up this time. This would be my sister, I thought, doing her thing, checking up on her younger sibling. She had behaved this way since I began dating guys, way back in the distant past, even before they had mobile phones.

I was wrong. Well, sort of. There was a message from her, but that had been much earlier in the day. She'd be worried I hadn't replied, so I did my duty and texted her back. I reassured her that I was fine, still compos mentis, and had enjoyed my first day at the resort. I wasn't about to share any information on my nocturnal misdemeanours with her right now. That required one of our traditional face-to-face conversations, held on such occasions, accompanied by a bottle of wine shared between us before she'd be in the mood for another of my confessionals. Click, send and done. Now, who was the other message from?

CHAPTER FOUR

I didn't recognise the number, but I did the attachments. So that's what happened last night. Wow! The signature and kisses told me that the photographs were either from Jade, Tom, or both. Further text messages with attachments arrived in rapid succession, and I soon guessed what was coming. The chronology of another head-spinning night in the life of Isabella and her newly acquired breakfast companions.

For his sins, Zach managed a brief turn of his head to see what I was doing. He sat up when he saw the disbelieving expression on my face as I flicked through the images. He leaned over my shoulder and then gave out a sigh of understanding. Standing now, he moved behind me for a better view, his hands falling on my shoulders, as he leant to kiss my neck and whispered in my ear. Then, with a sexy tone in his voice, he told me I had been a very naughty girl. My pussy twitched. I loved how easily he woke me up.

I finished swiping through the photos, stopping at various points to zoom in for more graphic detail of who exactly had done what and where. I particularly appreciated the close-up – I guess that would have been Jade taking the photo. And there I was, holding Zach and Tom's stiff cocks together on the tip of my tongue. Though, for the life of me, I was struggling to remember ever having done that. But something like that, surely you would not want to forget.

Thankfully, it seemed that I'd somehow managed to maintain

a certain degree of decorum. Everything is relative, right? No hardcore images of my body swamped beneath a writhing mass of fit, muscular men. Did I say thankfully? Not sure what I was thinking there!

The photographs helped jog my mind a little, and the fact that the alcoholic fog that was in my head when I woke up earlier was gradually clearing. And something else – another memory – was coming back. I swiped again through the photographs, this time looking for something particular. But there was nothing. No picture to verify this new memory. Had I imagined it? I had to find out.

I replied to the final tranche of adult images. "Hi, is that Jade? Or Tom? I pressed send, and in doing so, another wicked thought crossed my mind. I'd assumed it must be Jade or Tom. What if it wasn't? Oh, heck! Had someone else taken those pictures? One of the Italians, maybe? My pulse moved up a gear. Had I let myself go more than usual?

The seconds passed, becoming minutes. At least, it felt that way. I held my phone tight with both hands, watching and waiting for a reply. The screen began to fade as the screen saver kicked in, and still, I held it tight.

By this time, Zach had returned to his lounger, knowing never to interrupt when I was busy with my phone. He'd learnt that a long time ago. Our "no phones at the dinner table" meant we maintained a great rapport when we were doing things together. But when I had my phone in my hands, it meant "me time", and Zach respected that. It gave him the opportunity to watch porn whilst sitting next to me and getting off while I ignored him. Well, at least he believed that.

On the other hand, I liked that he was oblivious to my superpower - the ability to do more than one thing at the same time. Something he was incapable of, like most men. My peripheral vision meant I could text on my phone, keep an eye on the porn he was watching, enjoy the show he was putting on with his hand between his legs, and still have time to enjoy the wet tingly feeling between my legs. I never fail to be amazed at how men continually underestimate the female of the species.

Anyway, back to the photos, as I was about to lay down my phone, it came back to life with a message delivery notification. I tapped the icon to open the text and was greeted with an emoji kiss and smile. That was it. No name, no words, nothing. A moment later, a second message came through. This time I was greeted by Jade's broad, grinning face, holding on to a very wide-brimmed sun hat, with Tom's head leaning on her shoulder to get in the shot. It had been her sending the photos, thank goodness.

I replied, begging her to meet me for lunch on the main hotel terrazzo. She immediately agreed, so I grabbed my stuff, bent over to kiss Zach, and told him as I scurried away where I was going and not to expect me back any time soon. Time to get the full breakdown of what had happened the night before.

CHAPTER FIVE

Waiting for me at the table was Jade. I had no idea how she had managed to get there so quickly. She certainly was an interesting woman. I lay my bag beside the table and joined her. She was sipping what looked like a porn star martini, clearly enjoying playing with the straw as she did so. Her gaze held mine with her beautiful emerald eyes, peeking above the brim of her sunglasses, speaking to me without words. Her presence was reassuring as if she wanted to protect me. Those few extra years between us made trusting her easy to do. And at the same time, she was close enough in age for me to feel stirrings deep inside for this beautiful woman.

As she recounted what had transpired the evening before, I pieced together the fragments in my mind. We had done more than drink together. What she had done to me last night had made me see her in a different light. The way she touched was beyond sublime. How she moved between my legs had sent shudders through my body as no man had ever achieved. It was different, softer, more loving - two women expressing their desire tenderly, knowingly. I imagined that the rest of the holiday would be just like this – frisky thoughts, relaxation, more frisky thoughts. And seeing her sucking on the straw between her lips was enough to make me want more.

We chatted for an hour or so, swapping notes on the happenings of the previous twenty-four hours. Jade remembered more than I did, having the evidence to substantiate what went on, and she filled in the blanks in my memory. I asked her if the memory that had surfaced in my thoughts earlier had happened or if it was my imagination running away with me. I described the scenes as I remembered the fragments. She smiled and nodded as I recounted those events. I couldn't work out whether she was nodding in agreement or simply appreciating my fervid imagination.

"Darling," she began as I concluded my story. "Everything you have just described is, well." She paused for effect. "One hundred per cent, without exception, the truth, the whole truth, and nothing but the truth, so help you." She ended with a laugh and took a long suck on her straw.

Her confirmation of my memory gave me a rush of embarrassed arousal. Any more intense, and I think I would have fainted. I grabbed the chair arms and pulled my knees together in an emergency shut-down procedure. I stared at her, a look of astonishment on my face, and I remained that way for ages. She laughed once more.

When I finally regained a modicum of composure, I shook my head slowly as Jade continued to perform oral sex on her straw, sucking voraciously. She fixed me with her gaze - a look of satisfaction etched firmly on her face.

"Feeling better now, are we?" she asked softly.

She had confirmed that my recollections were fact. I had spent the better part of an evening enjoying the company of Zach and her partner, Tom, teasing them with my tongue, lips, fingernails, and goodness knows what else, taking all three of us well beyond common decency, savouring every inch of their bodies. From the photographs and our piecing together of the puzzle, I could see that Jade hadn't been any less active. We clearly performed well as a team.

Jade took her phone and swiped through the photos she had sent me earlier. Finally, she paused, studying the picture in front of her, before giving herself a virtual pat on the back. She held the phone in front of my face, arm outstretched, smiling silently. I took another deep breath.

In the first photo, my head was resting on the burgundy-red leather sofa in the hotel lounge. My hair was dishevelled. My makeup was a little worse for wear. To either side of me were Tom and Zach, both spent, heads on my shoulders, naked from the waist up – at least that's as far as I could tell from the photo. What made me gasp was the sight of far more than makeup on my face. Gifts, it seemed, from the two of them. I had been a very naughty person.

Could it get any worse? Absolutely! The next photo she produced continued the theme of Zach and Tom, with the addition of, I think, Luca underneath me. Either I was sitting on him, or he was nestled inside my butt. When had that happened? Tom and Zach were standing on the leather sofa, and I was greedily eating them both and enjoying Luca taking me from behind. Meanwhile, Jade was busy next to me with her two other male friends in a similar predicament. They reminded me of the straw she had been sucking earlier, though they were bigger than any straw I'd seen.

"And this, my darling, is the best of all". She had saved the best photo for last.

Somehow, from photograph number two to this one, I had lost all of my clothes, as had everyone else. Some Caribbean-looking guy had materialised from who-knows-where and was lying flat on his back. As he stretched across the sofa, I had straddled him, mounting him like a competition horse – and there appeared to be enough between my legs for him to qualify for that description. Luca had profited from my backside, bobbing up and down on the unknown guy's cock to rear-end me and had an expression of pure pleasure on his face. Meantime, I had somehow managed to take the whole of Jades' husband in my mouth, which I found impressive, given my general reluctance to deep throat. I'd had enough alcohol to bolster my confidence in that department. In the meantime, Zach was balls deep in Jade's ass. She had made the most of him and the two Italians. Presumably, Zach wasn't overly concerned about my gymnastics up to that point. Fair dues to him.

I slumped back in my chair, my head spinning. This was not the holiday I had expected; it was far better than I could have imagined. I felt the thrill of anticipation coursing through my veins and told myself I would not get drunk again. I wanted to remember every minute detail from this moment on. Six more days to go!

PLAN A

Sometimes you have to put yourself in the back seat when you have a friend in need. And if that literally means sitting in the back seat of a car while your friend rides in the front, then that's a sacrifice you're just going to have to make, at least until you get home.

CHAPTER ONE

Chrissie didn't want to stay late. It was already getting cold outside, and the thought of walking a mile home with the temperature dropping wasn't in the least bit appealing. But the pub was warm and inviting, with a big log fire burning bright, keeping the patrons nice and toasty, and she and her friends were having a wonderful time. Her best friend, Lisa, had decided to chat up the barman, and she was also the designated driver for the evening. So, it was a choice between waiting who knows how long for a lift or braving the dark street on her own. She decided it was best to hold on, knowing the weather forecast had promised a downpour that evening. So, she hunkered down with her gin and tonic and re-joined the conversation.

Meantime, Lisa was in full flow with Sam, the barman. Although born and raised in Oxford, his parents were from the Caribbean, and he carried himself with all the swagger that his tall, fit physique offered. Sam stood out in the middle of a group of pasty middle-aged regulars for his good looks and infectious smile. Tonight, he was having to deal with another middle-aged woman, albeit extremely attractive, flirting with him. The pub landlord had rules against this sort of thing, but, in any case, Sam enjoyed the banter and the attention received. And here was not one but two attractive MILFs, as he cheekily referred to them. Although he was a couple of years shy of forty, he found women older than him much more exciting and desirable.

A little after nine-thirty, Lisa's other bestie, Emily, walked in, half frozen and gloomy. With a quick scan of the local to find her friends, she headed to the bar, seating herself on the stool next to Lisa without saying a word. Chrissie, who saw her come in, already had an inkling of what was happening. It was becoming common knowledge that Emily and her boyfriend Gary were going through a prolonged rough patch. He'd been caught in flagrant with a married woman, making headline news in the pub for the past week. Unfortunately, Emily was the last to find out, making her feel embarrassed. Lisa broke the news to her once it was officially confirmed. It looked like it was the end of the road for Emily and Gary as a couple, not that he was worth it. Chrissie thought he looked creepy even when he was sober. Even so, it wasn't a very nice thing for him to cheat on her.

Lisa interrupted her conversation with Sam to check in with Emily. At the same time, Chrissie figured it would do no harm to show a bit of female solidarity, so she made her excuses and headed to the two friends, deep in conversation. Her near-empty glass of gin and tonic landed firmly on the bar top at the same time as her curvaceous bottom came to a cushioned landing on the stool to the other side of Emily. None of the women noticed Sam looking at them in an interested fashion.

It transpired that Chrissie had been spot on. Emily had fallen out massively with Gary and told him to get lost. He left her in the middle of town without considering how she would get home. So, she'd headed for the local on the off chance there'd be someone there whom she'd know and get a lift back home. Her timing was perfect as Lisa would have to give up on her attempts to seduce the barman, and maybe they'd all get home in time for one last glass of wine together. Unfortunately, Lisa was on a roll and was determined to have some fun and now maybe kill two birds with one stone. She didn't like to see her friend looking so glum and had quickly thought up a ruse to put a smile back on her face. Chrissie didn't know it then, but she was also about to become part of Lisa's mischievous plan.

Sam, standing only a couple of paces away from the three of them, was summoned by Lisa with short shrift and commanded to provide shots all around, a top-up G&T for her and Chrissie, and a double Porn Star Martini for Emily. The barman leapt into action, and within a minute, the three women were bonding with a ritualistic knocking back of their shots. Another three refills followed, and by eleven, they were decidedly more upbeat about the whole Gary affair, having attracted the attention of several men obviously married and in town on business. One by one, they let them down once they'd had a little flirty fun. In the meantime, they had noticed and commented on the way Sam kept looking their way with his characteristic smile. And as the number of regulars dwindled, Lisa raised the flirtation level aimed directly at Sam. Chrissie and Emily had sufficient alcohol in them by this late hour to decrease their unconscious bias towards being well-behaved. Blouse buttons on all three had slowly popped open as their combined cleavages provided onlookers with enough distraction to satisfy even the most innocent men. And Sam was all but innocent. As the evening went on, he edged closer to his side of the bar so they wouldn't notice the growing excitement in his trousers.

CHAPTER TWO

The bell rang for them to make their last orders, and it was only then that they realised that their designated driver, Lisa, was unfit to drive. That left them with the dilemma of how to get home. With nobody but them and the barmen still in the place, there was only one thing to do. Sam would have to step up and be their chauffeur for the night. He didn't need much persuasion as they leant forward onto the bar top, resting their now half-exposed breasts within inches of his reach. Sam took the key and moved to the bar's public side. As he approached them, Emily saw his semi-rigid mast poking under his trousers. She pointed straight at him and laughed, drawing the attention of the other two women to his current state of mind. They smiled at him voraciously. That just made him grow harder. This looked like it might be an eventful ride.

Lisa and Chrissie climbed into the back of the car, and Emily took the passenger seat next to Sam, who slid in, still aroused, and fumbled to start the engine. He wasn't familiar with the car, so Lisa leaned over from the back seat, took the key from his hand, and pressed the ignition button, ensuring that her ample breasts landed firmly against Sam's left cheek. She lingered long enough for him to realise it had been done on purpose. Up fluttered Sam's cock once more.

Lisa had wanted to get Sam to herself from the moment they'd arrived at the bar. Now she had him, but not all alone. Still, he seemed willing to go along with the three of them, and now he was in the car. Lisa planned to make sure Emily got the attention she deserved.

The journey back to Emily's house, though a short one, was nonetheless entertaining. At a certain point, Lisa tossed her house keys over to Emily, aiming them purposefully out of her reach, landing smack on the driver's side and hitting the floor between Sam's feet. Emily leant across to see where they'd ended up, and with the effects of the alcohol she'd consumed, she thrust her hand blindly between Sam's legs to try and grab the keys. Lisa leapt at the opportunity, leaning over from the rear passenger seat, placing her hand at the back of Emily's head, and pushing her downwards. Emily's face made a soft landing on Sam's crotch. She reacted to the sudden movement, trying to straighten herself. But only for a moment. The stiffness pushing through the fabric of his trousers persuaded her that this was a better way to get home. The last residual thoughts of her ex, Gary, were rapidly evaporating. She relaxed, and Lisa released her hold, seeing that Emily wasn't resisting.

Lisa sat back in her seat and looked toward Chrissie with a knowing wink while Sam took the whole thing in his stride. He definitely wasn't complaining about the sudden turn of events. A quick check in the rear mirror showed Lisa and Chrissie staring at him with mischief in their eyes. He was really starting to enjoy being the centre of so much attention and decided to take a longer route to their destination. No point in arriving too soon, he thought. He adjusted his mirror a little, just enough to improve the view of his backseat passengers. His side mirrors would do just fine for keeping an eye on the traffic.

Most likely, because of the company she had been keeping that evening, Emily decided that her day had been sufficiently crappy that a bit of self-indulgence was needed. She enjoyed nuzzling Sam's stiff tool and keeping it alert, but she hadn't eaten all day and felt peckish. Her hands moved forwards, taking hold of the zipper of his trousers. Sam would have to concentrate a little harder on where he was going, imagining where Emily intended to go. A slight tug and the zipper moved. A longer pull and down it came. At this point, Sam had to adjust his driving position, sliding himself forward just enough to give Emily some additional headroom. That was all she needed. Her left hand slipped inside his trousers, working out the fastest path to get hold of his now fully stiffened rod. Chrissie and Lisa leaned forwards to get a better view as Emily pulled his cock out from where he'd been keeping it warm. She had to move her head out of the way as it was quite a chunky specimen. Her two friends provided the sound effect of wicked delight as she pulled it into view.

CHAPTER THREE

The car turned right at the next junction and headed onto the dual carriageway. They were little more than ten minutes from dropping Emily off, the first stop on the journey home. Luckily, the roads were quiet at night, meaning Sam had more time to focus on what was happening inside the car rather than on the outside traffic.

One of Emily's less well-known skills was her ability to deep-throat any man. More often than not, Sam found that his girlfriends struggled to cope with the size of his manhood. But Emily wasn't one to turn down a challenge. She raised her head enough to take the tip of his cock between her lips, then opened wide. As she began to swallow him whole, Sam could do nothing but look down in amazement as he disappeared inside her mouth until her head rested on his lap. His head jolted in surprise, and he gave up trying to regain his composure as Lisa began to rhythmically move her head up and down sufficiently to make him throb uncontrollably.

Not one to be outdone, at this stage, Lisa made a strategic decision to up the ante in the car. She grabbed her handbag and rummaged for a few moments before fishing out a small vibrator. This one was for Chrissie. She dived into her bag again, pulling out the small toy's bigger cousin. Lisa never left home without at least one fully charged vibrator in her purse. You never knew when the need might arise.

Emily was busy enjoying her Big Mac, so she couldn't see what the other two were getting up to. Lisa looked straight into the mirror, catching Sam's gaze. As soon as they locked eyes, Lisa brought her vibrator up to her lips, licking the length of it without for a moment taking her eyes off Sam. Chrissie followed suit, and Sam was now a witness to these two stunning women flirting with him. But the best was yet to come.

Lisa shifted her weight forward and lifted her bottom off the seat just enough to slide her hands under her dress and ease down her knickers. She was impressed at how damp they'd gotten. She looked across to Chrissie, inviting her to do the same. Once removed, they tossed them nonchalantly over Sam's shoulders, landing right in front of him. He was sorely tempted to turn and look but had to resist, given his driving speed. And then he heard to sound of not one, but two vibrators being switched on. Even Emily listened to the sound and lifted her head to see what was happening. On seeing what her two friends were getting up to, she gave them a quick shrug, having decided that her meal was far more interesting, though she was getting thirstier by the minute. She hoped Sam would give her something to wet her lips soon.

Chrissie and Lisa leaned back, perching their feet on the backs of the driver and passenger seats, and slid their dresses above their waists. At this point, the whole scene was getting way too much for Sam, who prided himself on being able to drive in a straight line. The view in his mirror left nothing to the imagination as he watched both women play with themselves, touching and toying with their glistening wet pussies as he drove through the night. Their hands crossed over, and they played with each other, fingers alternating between dipping into their wet wells and returning to their mouths. Eventually, Sam could take it no longer.

Emily's house was just ahead and was all he needed as he slowed down and turned off the main road onto her driveway, hitting the brakes and coming to a stop. His hand shot across to his seat belt buckle, and he released it. Moments later, he arched back as Lisa took him to the edge of ecstasy with a long, high-pressure lick from the base of his cock to the tip. Finally, he was pushed over the edge with a final flutter from her tongue. He came hard and fast. Copious amounts of his cum soaked Emily's face, overshooting the mark, and landing on Chrissie's knee. Emily took him once more in her mouth as he continued to gush, holding on to as much of his juice as she could. She waited until he had finished, pulling herself away from him as slowly as she could manage.

By this stage, both Lisa and Chrissie were ready to explode, and the sight of Sam releasing all over Emily gave them the push they needed, with Lisa gushing uncontrollably as she often did. Their pleasure lasted for several seconds until the contractions subsided, and they relaxed, both exhausted.

Emily was staring at them both, her cheeks puffed up, lips closed tight, as she held on to Sam's creamy present. She mumbled unintelligibly at them, pointing to her mouth. There was nothing else to do but for the two back seat passengers to straighten themselves up, lean forward and touch lips with Emily. Their tongues unfolded, Emily slowly eased open her lips, and the three of them lapped up the warm gift that Sam had given them.

They adjusted themselves and piled out of the car. Sam looked puzzled. Wasn't he meant to drop them off at their respective houses? Lisa leaned in and winked at Sam as she waved the car key in her hand. Just then, it dawned on Sam that he had no way to get home.

"Coming to join us, Sam?" asked Lisa. But, of course, that had been her plan all along.

FLASH PHOTOGRAPHY

Isabella has high standards on who she considers acceptable as a potential "friend with benefits". Not many potential candidates pass the test of good looks, great personality, and for men, a decent sized toolbox. Finding one is quite a challenge, but finding two who come as a package deal, what are the chances? Occasionally, Isabella strikes gold, as in this case.

CHAPTER ONE

I leave it to Zach to do the heavy lifting when trawling through the dozens of men and occasional couples who put themselves forward as potential friends with benefits. After a year of setting up our profile on one of those websites for naughty singles and couples, he'd reviewed hundreds of potential candidates. Unfortunately, only a few dozen made it through the first round to land on my screen for review. Of those, probably half were immediately discarded. Of the remainder that made it to the interview, only a handful were invited to meet in person. Many of them were a waste of time, finding every excuse under the sun for not attending the mandatory social. The best excuse I heard was that of a guy who couldn't come because he had to look after his dog.

Now, I admit to having a soft spot for Italian men, probably because I know very few, one actually, and his name happens to be Zach, my lover. Well, if this one is amazing, who's to say that all Italian men aren't at least half as good as him, in which case, result! So, it was the strangest thing when not one, and not even two, but three Italian men contacted us within a day of each other. Although, in fairness, two of those guys came as a single package. Now that was a novelty. So, after a year of famine on the Italian front, I found myself with a potential feast in the making. Just in time for Christmas too!

After a slow start and an even slower summer, things started to pick up around November time. As this was the first full year I had been involved in the "lifestyle", it was quite a learning curve. It was the same for Zach, too, even though he had previously been exposed to such things. Who knew, for example, that swingers tend to hibernate in the summer months? It may have something to do with the extended school holidays. Or maybe, like vampires, swingers don't like it when it's too bright and sunny outside. Whatever the real reason, when the clocks went back in October, there was a significant uptick in single men and couples signalling their willingness to play.

It was mid-November when Zach messaged me to say that an Italian guy had contacted us. I immediately perked up. After the ritual backwards and forwards between Zach and the new arrival, a facial picture of the candidate popped up. Not bad. I'd say seven out of ten, which on the Isabella scale is slightly more than acceptable, if not exceptional.

At this stage, it's worth explaining my selection criteria, as I set the bar quite high on what I consider an acceptable standard in my friends with benefits. Men must, in most cases, have a full head and no facial hair. The only exceptions are men with exceptional good looks and physique or, as I discovered, Italians. I also require them to be reasonably fit, with pleasant-looking tackle, not too big (I suppose) and not too small (I'm sure). Age, dress sense and intelligence are other significant factors when deciding whether or not they get through to the video-chat stage. Six out of ten don't make it through first contact on the screen.

I digress. My first Italian suitor, being a seven out of ten, got through the first and second stages of assessment, and we arranged a social meeting to see how things developed.

All good so far. Then, the next day, Zach messages me with the news that another two Italian men had contacted us, this time coming as a package and both straight. It was beginning to sound a lot like Christmas!

Having done a similar vetting exercise, I confess that all three were in the seven to eight out of ten range. Not bad for two days of reviewing applications. Then came the surprise bonus; one of the three was a professional photographer specialising in boudoir photography. Oh my god, I was definitely going to have a few exciting weeks ahead. So, I now had Aaron, the single guy, Marco, the photographer, and his friend Davide. I'm not saying out of the three, one was sexier than the others, as they may read this, but each of them had something yummy that the other two didn't have. Oh, and goodness me, none of them had shared any pictures of their nether regions. Now that made a refreshing change. You've got to hand it to the Italians; they sure know how to woo a woman.

CHAPTER TWO

Within a few days, I connected with all three on one of the chat apps I use. Telegram, in case you're wondering. All three were, for unrelated reasons, in Italy at the time we made first contact. We arranged to meet all three of them a couple of weeks later, as they came from London. Talk about coincidences upon coincidences! Zach and I had organised a day out at a theatre in London, an hour from where we lived. It made sense to arrange a mid-morning social with the single guy and then separately with the couple, as the Jersey Boys matinee performance we had booked to see didn't start until 2:30 pm.

In the meantime, the fact that Marco was a photographer, specialising in using his own words, "chiaroscuro" (dark and light, aka black and white) photos, excited Zach and me. So I sent Marco and Davide some boudoir photos I'd taken earlier this year. When Marco commented that I didn't need his professional skills as I already had my collection, I quickly corrected him, suggesting I wanted some racier boudoir photographs. That perked him up. Zach and I had a chat about this, and as we'd bought several sexy lingerie sets as well as a few more BDSM-leaning outfits over the past year, we decided that I would lay them all out on the bed and photograph them. We could then share the photos with Marco and Davide, and I could spend the fortnight before meeting them to discuss what to wear and what poses to strike.

At this point, you'd be correct to infer that the single guy, Aaron, was taking a back seat to my attention, predominantly focused on having fun with Marco, Davide, and of course, Zach. That's not to say I was going to ignore Aaron, absolutely not, but needs must, and with everything else going on in my life, I have precious little time to focus on more than one thing at a time.

I'd previously only had a couple of experiences paying with two men who knew each other. On the first occasion, it was pleasant enough, although their average score was six and a half out of ten. The second time, I was in a room with three guys, a girl, and Zach. It wasn't something I wanted to repeat with people who, for the most part, were first-time meets. It ended awkwardly, and I'd not spoken to any of them since. So, meeting up with two guys who came as a package was going to be a new experience for me, and with them being Italian two, I was full of anticipation.

Now, if you get the wrong idea about me, let me stress that I don't jump into bed with anyone. I prefer to have had at least one video conversation with men first and a social meeting to follow up. Although, given how precious my time is, more often than not, the social, if successful, usually follows immediately with an erotic encounter of the close kind. The exception to this rule is when Zach and I go to a club for fun. Let's say that, for us, a club is like going shopping. I start with window shopping, and if I see anything I like, I can try it on for size. Mainly I go home empty-handed, having tried a few things, but found nothing I fancy. On odd occasions, I swap notes and follow up with repeated fittings, so to speak.

Although we had initially planned to arrive in London at around ten o'clock, grab some brunch, and do a little pre-Christmas shopping before heading to the theatre, we had to make a slight modification to accommodate our unexpected guests. Zach booked a day-use hotel a few hundred yards from the theatre. He's a very effective personal assistant to me. We had the option to cancel free of charge up to the day of arrival. So, I had options available depending on how the interviews with one or all of them went. So now, there was little left for me to do than keep my three potential new toys warmed up for two weeks and open up a few conversations and photographs to warm me up nicely. During that time, I discovered the likes and dislikes of both me, though in truth, Marco was by far the more talkative. Davide had a more regimented work routine, probably an office job, though he never mentioned what he did for a living. Marco took photographs and seemed to be well travelled. Their desires would come to the surface a little at a time over the coming months.

CHAPTER THREE

By the time our London trip had arrived, I had passed two delightful weeks flirting with all three Italians. For his sins and in the guise of my personal assistant, Zach had the task of managing my inbox during this period. He does an excellent impression of me when needed, too! We'd discussed various scenarios, and given that we probably had four hours available, including a coffee social, we decided to meet Marco and Davide, pushing Aaron back to a later date. I prefer quality over quantity, and with Zach in the mix, too, three Italians were plenty for me to get my hands on at any given time.

Another thing we'd done in the lead-up to our rendezvous, Zach more than me, was to spend some time searching for erotic boudoir photographs. His idea was to come up with a couple of dozen poses I could strike as part of a "scenario" to play out with the three of them. I extended his search criteria to include a man and woman in the photo shots. We ended up with plenty of ideas. All we had to do was take our digital camera with us.

We'd arranged to meet Marco and Davide at a coffee shop near our hotel at ten o'clock on Thursday. When we arrived, they were already waiting for us. That was a nice touch. Now, I have to explain that in the confusion of our initial conversations, Zach mentioned that he had lived and worked in Italy for several years. Marco took it to mean that I had been there and assumed I understood some Italian. As a result, to avoid embarrassment, I received a crash course in essential Italian from Zach in the fortnight leading up to our meeting. By essentials, I mean how to say yes, no, more, and enough. According to Zach, that, plus a smattering of "you are gorgeous", was all I needed to get by.

For those of you who are interested in meeting Italian men, the literal translations are SI for yes, NO for no (that's easy), ANCORA for more, and BASTA for enough. I'll leave it up to you to work out how to say "you're gorgeous" in Italian. Never let it be said that I don't put effort into the things I do, especially when they lead to something pleasurable.

One thing that Italian men do well is the bit where they greet you. Both of them saw us arriving, stood up, and placed their hands tastefully around my waist as they pulled me in for a kiss on both cheeks. Nothing inappropriate, simply charming. The few seconds I had, from seeing them to standing in front of them, were sufficient to reassure me that they were both at least seven out of ten, a good start.

We settled down for a coffee, which they insisted on buying. I found it quite exciting to meet two strangers who were comfortable in each other's presence and were doing their best to impress me without any hint of competitiveness. It felt like they knew how to play as a team. They soon discovered that Zach was the one with Italian heritage, which made for a little gentle banter as the three of them exchanged a few words in Italian that I did not understand. Their looks toward me as they spoke made it more than obvious who they were talking about. Now, ordinarily, I might be bothered if others were talking about me behind my back. But, in this case, the sounds of their voices and that velvety Italian language made me want more. They could have continued that way for the whole time we were going to be together, and I would have been in heaven. Sadly, they reverted to good old English after a few moments. Still, these two had a sexy accent, whatever language they spoke.

Conscious of our precious little time until the doors opened at the theatre, I took the unusual step of quickly downing my coffee. After a little more than fifteen minutes, I put my cup down and squeezed Zach's hand, our signal to say, "I'm in". I didn't need to ask twice, as he immediately drank up and said something in Italian to the other two. They followed suit, at the same time smiling in my direction. We rose in unison from the table and gathered our belongings before leaving the coffee shop and heading toward the hotel. My high heels clicked on the paving stones as Marco and Davide accompanied me on either side, with Zach walking beside the three of us. Within a couple of minutes, we'd arrived.

No matter how often Zach and I had done this, getting through a hotel reception with one or more guests in tow was always the most stressful part of any encounter. We were always concerned that the receptionist would call us to a halt and question what we were doing. So, we did our best to find hotels with an ample reception area and, ideally, a bar or other seating, which meant we could give the impression of being there just for drinks. Then we would have someone sneak everyone into the lift without giving the game away to the hotel staff. Usually, that was much easier said than done. In this case, the hotel reception was right next to the main entrance, so there was no chance of sneaking them in. So, we enacted plan B, with Zach checking in and the three of us putting on our best poker faces and walking past Zach and the rather attractive receptionist. We made it safely past them both, with Zach using his charm to distract her from our presence. He did an excellent job of it, and we reached the bar as I made a mental note of the lift location for our next manoeuvre.

Marco had some essential photography equipment in his bag. I had a different collection of items in mine. The combination of the two was something I was looking forward to trying out. In the preamble to our meeting, we had discussed all manner of things, one of which was my growing list of fantasies. As Marco was a professional boudoir photographer, you can imagine what naughty thoughts were going through my mind. I had every intention of exploiting his skills and those of his friend to my gratification and also walking out with a nice set of photographs.

CHAPTER FOUR

Zach joined us, having checked in, and passed the key card to Marco. He and Davide grabbed their things and headed to the lift, keeping a low profile to avoid any funny looks from the sexy woman behind the desk. They needed a few minutes to set up their gear in the hotel room. Meanwhile, Zach and I laughed and fumbled with each other like two teenagers, despite being well past our prime. On second thoughts, I was beginning to enter my prime, so scrub that last sentence. Even though it was still not eleven in the morning, I needed a Pinot Grigio with soda to calm my nerves. That was another thing I'd been unable to stop feeling, despite no longer being new to this kind of transgression. Some things never change. Zach strolled across to the bar and ordered a large glass of pale nerve relaxant in a wine glass.

Although I had a general sense of what he'd organised for the day, only Zach knew the detail. We enjoy doing this thing where he writes down specific instructions or guidance for me and others before sealing them in red envelopes. I only know what I'm to do when I open the envelope. In this case, he'd already told me I was to open it when I was in the hotel room, not before, and only once I had changed into something more appropriate for the occasion. The other thing Zach and I agreed upon was that he would instruct me on what to wear. These acts were our nod to his dominance and my submissiveness.

While I was waiting for Zach to return with my drink, the two Italians returned, smiling and chatting as they approached. I was seated at the centre of a long sofa. They sat on either side of me as if they'd done this a thousand times before. Their hands fell upon my knees, and I immediately felt a jolt of excitement run up from my knees to my stomach. Well, maybe a little lower than that. I've always had a soft spot for the sensation that comes from sitting between two attractive men while they've got their clothes on. Call me a snob if you will, but I find men to be far more interesting and exciting when they are made to be charming and flirty. Once their clothes come off, they always seem to have just one thing in mind, but when they are dressed, then I get all the eye candy I could wish for while they try their best to turn me on. Of course, I try not to let on just how turned on I already am as I lap up their attention.

Now, although I was as nervous as the first time I'd found myself in this situation, I now had a little more understanding of what to do and, in particular, what I wanted. From my seated position, I pushed myself back into the deep sofa, leaning against it so my body went from vertical to half-horizontal. I learned that my legs naturally spread a little when leaning back. Their hands, already on my legs above my knees, slid towards the hem of my stockings. Their reaction was instantaneous as they both tightened their grip on the soft flesh of my upper thighs. They may have been worried they would lose their hold on me.

They both leaned in as I shifted backwards, maintaining a firm hold on me and discovering the warmth of my inner legs. I do believe I was pleasantly damp down there, having been sitting with my legs closed in the preceding minutes. The sounds coming out of their mouths at that moment were enough to convince me that they were enjoying themselves, which in turn, just made me warm up even more. I may have been a little nervous, but my nerves were already passing as I flirted with the two of them. I did what I'd learnt to do in my conversations with Zach. I stretched both arms out and lay them on their legs, right where the trouser leg meets the inner thigh. I may have accidentally brushed over their inner thighs as I did so, but just with my fingertips. There was no point in being utterly outrageous at this stage. As I did so, I looked into their eyes, first

Marco, then Davide. They reciprocated with a tighter grip on my legs, and I'm pretty sure they both moved higher up as their fingers passed from nylon stocking to naked flesh, crossing the lace barrier that divided the two.

Zach arrived with a glass of Pinot and a sexy smile. He enjoyed seeing me being the centre of others' attention. We all sat patiently and spoke for another minute or two as I sipped my wine. Then, Zach slipped his hand into his inside jacket pocket and extracted three red envelopes, one each for Marco, Davide, and me. That was my cue to stand, pick up my bag, glass of wine, and the key card resting on the table. I wriggled past them and headed for the lift.

The cardinal rule that Zach and I had, and that others were required to adhere to, was that the instructions each of us received in our red envelopes were sacrosanct. We had to follow them to the letter. But, of course, that didn't mean stifling our creativity; instead, they were guidelines for us to follow, like a script in a film. As the lift carried me to my destination, I wondered what those instructions were for each of us.

I swiped the key card and entered the room. The curtains had been drawn, and the room bathed in the soft glow of bedside lamps and the photographer's lighting. Zach's digital camera was seated on a large tripod in one corner. A bottle of champagne was chilling in an ice bucket on the desk. Soft music was playing in the background. I checked out the bathroom and saw it had a walk-in shower. The bedroom was an executive suite with a large sofa and a king-size bed. Overall, I was pleased with the size and layout of the room, as there is nothing worse than finding yourself in a less-than-premier room when you're planning on indulging in an erotic fantasy. Sometimes the little things make all the difference. I was hoping there wouldn't be too many little things on the menu today.

After freshening up, I took my time to get dressed. This part was always the preamble to my excitement as I still had no idea what was in the envelope. I emptied my bag of its contents, including the clothes I'd been asked to pack and a few things that Zach had added. As I was already wearing stockings and suspenders, I removed my shoes, dress, and underwear. In place of them, I slid the black and red satin and lace corset and crotchless knickers. I sprayed perfume all over and replaced my shoes with expensive red heels. My black seamed stockings and matching suspender belt completed the look. I placed the complementary wrist and ankle restraints, collar with chain, jewelled butt plug, and black silk blindfold on the bed. The horse crop had already flipped out when I'd emptied the bag. I placed it beside the other trinkets. Next, I put my two favourite toys, number seven and nine, as I called the two pink dildos, in reference to their length, and carefully positioned them on the bedside cabinet. I finished my glass of wine, retrieved the red envelope from Zach, and nervously opened it. I read slowly, twice through, to ensure I understood everything. Then, I had one final task to complete before enacting the instructions. I sent a text message to Zach, letting him know I was ready. It was time for lights, cameras, action!

CHAPTER FIVE

The background music had been carefully studied to dull my hearing to the sound of anyone entering the room, making it harder for me to discern if one or more footsteps were approaching. The silk blindfold kept me in the dark about who he, she, or they might be. All I could make out was the bedroom door opening. Several seconds later, it closed once more.

My instructions had been explicit. I moved the chair to the centre of the room, seating myself on it, facing away from the door, toward the window. I fitted the wrist and ankle restraints, leaving them loose at the other end. Then I applied the blindfold, and I was ready. Several seconds after the door closed, I felt the first touch of skin against mine. My wrists were taken in turn and tied behind, around the back of the chair. Next, they spread my legs, my feet shifted, and I could feel the two restraints around my ankles tied to the legs of the chair. I strained to hear whether there were one, two, or more men in the room, but it was hard to tell for sure.

Now I could hear movement further away and the sound of the camera being turned on. I felt the brightness of the photographer's light being pointed straight at me, the heat rising just a degree or two as it warmed my near-naked flesh. The lamp further blinded me to everything around me. I was as submissive as possible, chained to this chair, my legs open to the attention of whoever was in the room. I felt my body stiffen and the excitement grow. Then, the click of a shutter rang in my ears. The first photograph had been taken. I could feel my nipples harden. Who was watching me? What were they doing? I could sense that they were taking their time, enjoying the moment. I wasn't yet in a rush, but I could feel my pulse quicken. What was next?

Then, the unexpected happened. I recognised the feel of ropes passing around my upper thighs, around each leg, just above my knees. Confident hands were at work, wrapping the rope around one leg, then the other. They tightened slightly, taking grip, and then slowly, purposefully, the two ropes pulled my legs, spreading them further apart, my knees distancing themselves one from the other until they were as wide as I could stretch, and still they pulled a fraction more. I tried to resist a little, then relented, wanting to see where this was going. The tension on my inner thighs was palpable. Then, as the ropes were anchored, I felt someone behind me resting a hand on each shoulder, holding me gently in place and another shutter click.

As I sat there, I could feel the heat of the light against my moistening skin. The first beads of sweat coalesced all over my body. The first drop ran along my forehead, cascading onto my cheek, followed by another. I remained still, enjoying the sensation of the unknown as the temperature rose in the room. I already knew there was more than one man in the room. The hands on my shoulders and the click of the camera confirmed that. The only question remaining was whether all three of them were there. I already imagined they were all with me, as they wouldn't want to miss this, would they? In answer to any lingering doubt, I felt the other one's hands lay on my wide, spread legs, softly touching me just above my knees. I tried to imagine where he might be. Was he standing or crouching, perhaps even kneeling in front of me? Another click, another photograph.

The man before me made the first move. His hands began to climb my legs, along my thighs, edging closer and closer to the belt that held my stockings in place. I played again, tugging my body to feign resistance, though I was all but resistant to his moves. His hands slid inwards and upwards, now firmly against the insides of my thighs, coming ever closer to the lace edges of my crotchless knickers. The heat was rising outside from the hot light and the feeling of restraint and submission. The hands on my shoulders moved forwards and down, descending toward my breasts, and two more hands advanced from below. Then, one of those hands, to my left, from above, stopped beneath my chin and raised my head upwards, tilting it backwards. His lips met mine in a passionate but unrecognisable kiss. He wasn't Zach; I was sure of that. At the same time, the other man's hands halted their advance, mere centimetres from my underwear, pushing me gently apart. I was taken by the kiss and strong hands upon my breasts and only realised what the other was doing when it was upon me. He was undoubtedly kneeling in front of me. I knew that from the angle that his lips and tongue came into contact with my underwear. His lips pressed against my body for mere moments before his tongue began a journey of delicious exploration. I let out a sigh as the camera clicked once more.

The more their tongues played with my body, the more pleasure I gained. The simple delight of gentle toying did more than I'd imagined, and when they finally ended this game, I knew I wanted more. The restraints around my legs were undone, and my hands were released from their binds. The blindfold remained, though not for long, as they led me to the sofa, seating me in the centre, my hands by my sides. I could hear the sound of movement, though it took me a few moments to realise what it was. The photographer's light was re-positioned, as were the tripod and camera. But, the photo shoot was far from over.

Then I heard the unmistakable sound of clothes being discarded. To my left and right, I could hear them undressing. In front of me, more sounds of clothes falling away. All three were readying themselves. As I waited, silence descended once more, to be broken by the sound of two men seating themselves on either side of me. I could feel their nakedness as they sat close beside me, my hands in contact with their skin. I followed the instructions I'd been given and did not move at all. That was until they took my hands and guided them towards their eager bodies, resting one hand on each of them against the inside of their thighs. I could sense their movements and the shifting of their bodies as they stroked themselves as their hands explored my body intimately and delicately. Fingers caressed my lips, daring to enter me for just a moment, feeling the dampness of my body grow stronger by the second. Their movements grew stronger as they became harder, until first one, then the other took my hand and placed it there. I could feel them throbbing with desire. I wondered what the third was doing, the one in front of me. Then I heard the shutter click once more before the lights came on at last.

As I stroked my two companions, the third approached and pushed my legs apart. He reached forward and released my silken ties; the blindfold fell from my eyes. Zach stood before me, naked except for his unbuttoned white shirt, aroused and full of desire in his eyes. Marco and Davide sat beside me, and I could finally see what I had already felt, all three wanting me. I began with Zach, kissing him deeply, before turning my attention first to one, then the other of the two by my sides. I leaned forward and down, taking each one in my mouth, deep and long, enjoying the feeling. I was pleased with how hard they all were, so often a disappointment, I found. This time though, they were as stiff as could be, and my mind told my body to react in kind. I felt myself grow moist in record time. And then we played in every way you could imagine, first one, then the other, then together. I took two of them together, first here, then there. And finally, all three at once, as they pushed deep inside. On my knees on the sofa, with my legs in the air, they took me every way they could, following the script Zach had prepared as best they could. I didn't need to follow any script; I improvised. And every minute, I heard the shutter click again. They'd set it to automatically capture every moment we shared. It was the best photoshoot of my life.

FIRST TIME LOVER

In reality, a first encounter is not always as memorable as you might hope. But, with a bit of forethought and a good deal of preparation, it is also true that sometimes the first time can be truly amazing.

CHAPTER ONE

"Who is it?" I asked.

"My name is Jordan, and you are Isabella, right?" came the reply.

My heart was beating like a drum. I opened the door ajar cautiously, never having met this man in person before this moment.

"Hello, Isabella"

He smiled as we came into each other's line of sight. He was quite delightful to look at, and what perfect white teeth. It took me two seconds to scan the man before me. Tall, but not overly so; dressed like a trendy forty-year-old should, neither too casual nor too smart. A nice crisp white shirt unbuttoned just enough to seem less formal than would otherwise have been the case. As my eyes descended and reascended, I noted the reasonably flat stomach – always a turn on, and the broad shoulders. To complete the look, a fashionably stubbled look, short enough not to inflame my sensitive skin, and a full head of hair. He easily scored 8 out of 10 on the Isabella Spice scale. I opened the door wide.

"Please, do come in", I uttered in the best put-on, sultry voice I could muster in the circumstances.

I looked him in the eyes as he struggled to keep his focus on mine and not let his gaze drift downwards to take in the rest of me, suitably attired for the occasion. Although it was early evening, I'd decided on a short burgundy dress which wrapped itself deliciously around my size 12 curves, providing just enough of my flesh to be on show whilst maintaining a refined look. Black stilettos raised me a good three inches, and there were still a few more between us in height. I prefer to be looking slightly upward when I kiss.

I stepped back as the door opened to allow him space to enter. As he did so, he casually pressed the remote in his hand, and the lights on his steel blue Porsche flashed as it locked. You can tell a lot about a man by his car. This one was sleek and expensive. As he stepped into the atrium, I closed the door, checking him out from the back. This time I was done in less than a second as I clocked his nicely curved backside, shapely and firm. Amongst my pet hates are men, or women, with too little or much in the rear department. I like my men to be well-proportioned in every respect. Jordan was scoring high in every category so far. He turned to face me.

"Can I just say Zach wasn't exaggerating when he described you?"

"Thank you" was all I could come up with at short notice.

I regained my composure after a moment.

"I think he did a good job of understating you, too," I responded. "You are definitely my kind of man."

We smiled once more at each other, a quite sensual pause in our somewhat brief introductory conversation. But then, this was the first time I had agreed to allow a stranger to visit me, albeit after a long preamble of chat, video calls, and a personal meeting between him and my partner, Zach. My outstretched arm signalled to him that we should move to the lounge. He took my simultaneous nod to mean that he should lead the way, which he did. I followed.

"Please, sit down," I said, "and what can I get you to drink?"

"If you have a whisky, I'll take one straight, thank you", came the immediate response as he descended into the broad-backed, burgundy-red leather sofa. It was the one that Zach and I had chosen, especially for the lounge. An old-fashioned three-seater formed the centrepiece of our slightly art-deco-style layout. The dim lighting from our tabletop lamps cast just the right amount of shadow in the room, giving it a sense of decadence. I watched him sink into the leather gracefully, his arms spreading to the side and back to ensure he opened up his whole body to the room. The buttons on his shirt went taught as his shoulders made contact with the sofa's backrest. It was a tight, figure-hugging shirt, showing off his fit torso. Well, that was a nice view to take in.

I turned and walked across to the drinks cabinet, ensuring I moved my thighs in rhythm with my steps. I read somewhere that walking with a wiggle is attractive, and I was keen to see if it worked in practice. I turned my head as I reached the drinks, just in time to see his gaze completely fixated on my backside. Mission accomplished, then! I waved a couple of bottles of whisky in the air, inviting him to choose between them. He went for the more expensive option. I picked up two tumblers and the bottle, returning to the sofa. As I approached, he stood up and reached across to assist. I made a mental note that he had good manners as well as looks. He was well on his way to reaching 8.5 out of 10. As he took the glasses and bottle from my hand, a little voice in my head alerted me that one of my hold-ups was slipping slightly. The silver bands holding up my seamed stockings were getting loose. I wasn't going to let the opportunity slip, either. As he bent slightly to place the drinks on the coffee table, I leaned forward, hitched up the front of my already relatively short dress, and provided him with a front-row view of my upper thigh. I wrapped my fingers around the elastic hem of first one hold-up, then the other, pulling on them to readjust their position. He remained unmoving as he absorbed what was happening right in front of him. Then, for good measure, I turned my back to him, raised the rear of my dress almost to my backside, and asked him to check if my seams were straight.

"Absolutely", he replied, almost spluttering as he did so.

He tried to clear his throat as I turned around with a wicked smile and suggested he pour our drinks before he choked. He laughed out loud, having regained his composure even faster than I'd done earlier. I raised an eyebrow to give him the sense that I was in control. Of course, I wasn't even the slightest bit in control, but I wasn't going to let him know.

CHAPTER TWO

We settled side by side on the leather sofa and spent a good twenty minutes in polite, if slightly flirtatious, conversation. I call this moment the seduction phase, where two strangers who clearly find each other physically attractive try to discover if they connect in a slightly more intimate, almost intellectual way. Zach and I had often debated what it was that made an encounter more than just a simple sexual act, and the answer was always the same; there needs to be a connection between the mind as well as the body. Finding such a connection with others was the most challenging aspect of our shared passion. We found it somewhat easier to find individuals who were compatible with us. Couples seemed to be just too hard. The odds of matching the two of us with another couple and everyone liking each other in body and spirit seemed a bridge too far.

Within twenty minutes, Jordan and I were comfortable and relaxed in the other's company. We weren't a perfect match, I had Zach for that, but we found enough common points of interest to make the conversation flow without too much effort. A little blue light in the corner of the room gave me the added reassurance that I was safe to do as I pleased in the presence of this not-so-new stranger. I decided it was time for him to take the initiative. Up to that point, I had maintained a certain distance between the two of us, though in truth, as the minutes passed, the gap between us dwindled until there was barely an inch or two separating our thighs by the time we had finished our second whisky. I eased my legs a fraction apart, just enough for my naked knee to brush against his. Thank goodness, his reaction was near instantaneous. His thigh moved just enough to press against mine – first contact. His nearer arm moved simultaneously around the sofa's backrest to wrap itself around me. I leaned forward to place my drink on the table, and as I straightened back upright, his arm was around my shoulder. He pulled me closer, our faces now much closer, and his bright blue eyes looked passionately into mine. We continued talking, this time, with bated breath, as we could feel the other's pulse racing.

I leaned forward, barely able to resist. I could feel the heat rising on my skin. The deep musky scent of his body making my senses spin with the urge to throw caution to the wind. But I resisted. He had to make the first move as this was one contest I would win. He had to show me he wanted me. I didn't have to wait too long. Once he'd laid down his glass, he had a free hand to do with as he pleased. It came to rest on my knee, gently caressing the expensive nylon that clad my legs. They had been a gift from Zach, with a naughty look in his eyes when he said they were for a special occasion. I couldn't resist looking away from Jordan at that moment toward the little blue light. I stared straight at it for a few moments before turning my gaze to the hand on my leg, gently caressing me. He had made the first move in a little under thirty minutes. Not bad going. I was starting to feel more confident.

I adjusted my position slightly so our bodies could come more fully into contact. The feeling of direct physical contact with a body against mine makes me want to wrap my arms around them. I enjoy being hugged and hugging, almost like giving and receiving reassurance, a moment of acknowledgement between two people that all will be well. Maybe he would hug me, and perhaps he wouldn't. I could only wait and see as he continued to caress my leg gently, almost as if he were wondering what to do next. I shouldn't have doubted his intentions, as moments later, he leaned forwards, closing the space between us to mere millimetres. His eyes met mine once more as he paused, his lips a fraction away from mine. Would he kiss me? He waited, seeking approval in my eyes. I gave him the sign by not backing away even a fraction. I held my position and held his gaze. He wasted no time in recognising my signals, and moments later, I tasted his lips on mine. A firm, passionate kiss, which within seconds transformed into tongues exploring one other, mouths parted with a longing to begin their exploration deep into each other. Our journey into each other had begun.

My desire for men is on three levels: their attractiveness, emotional intelligence, and ability to satisfy me. The first two were relatively easy to assess. The third aspect required a more intimate experience, one I was ready and willing to undertake at this point. As we kissed, his arms wrapped around me, I took a deep breath and leaned into him. Doing so, I had to regain some balance, purposefully shifting my hand, so it landed on the uppermost part of his thigh. It was a perfect touchdown as I could feel something hard beneath his trousers at the outer limits of my finger. We continued to kiss passionately, and Jordan wasn't anyone's fool as he immediately recognised what I was doing and edged himself even closer. Again, my hand shifted to accommodate his movement, this time falling directly on his stiffness. My mind did a quick calculation, and he moved instantly from 8.5 to 9.0 on my scale. I squeezed what was, at this point, beneath my hand, for good measure. Again, there was an instant and positive reaction as I felt him throb nicely.

After a minute or more, I had to come up for breath. I hadn't kissed so passionately for quite a while. Perhaps I'm exaggerating, as Zach and I had spent that morning in bed making love for well over an hour. But it had been a while since I'd kissed a stranger so passionately. I pushed Jordan back and smiled, blowing a breath as if to say wow, that was good. Then I leaned back, straightening my dress with my hands. I kept eye contact for a few moments, allowing him to take in the view from his position on the sofa. Then I turned my back to him and pointed to the zip on the back of my dress.

"Would you mind?" I asked innocently, repeatedly pointing at the zip catch.

"Oh, of course", he replied, standing swiftly in response.

I felt his firm hands take the dress and zipper, and in the otherwise silent room, we both heard the sound of my dress zip slowly descending. He took his time, which was a nice touch. When it reached its final destination, he released the zip catch, and I felt his hands on my shoulders. He eased the shoulder straps apart, and the dress fell deftly to the ground, exposing my lingerie-clad body to his gaze. His hands remained on my shoulders for a moment. Although my back was to him, I could feel the penetrating look he was giving me as he took in my curves, wrapped in expensive black lace lingerie. His hands descended along my back until he reached the curve of my waist. It rested there for a moment before he stepped forward, pressing himself against my bottom and back. I could feel his excitement against my butt cheeks. He held me tight and kissed my neck, nibbling gently. I began to suspect that Zach had provided him with a Michelin tour guide to Isabella. He had nailed the right moves.

Eventually, I tired of this unseen attention and turned to face my handsome stranger. He cast his eyes upon my curves, taking in the frontal perspective. I could see he was impressed. I could also see that his excitement had taken on quite large proportions. I didn't want to waste any more time. We kissed once more, and then I took a step back, reaching for his shirt buttons and making light work of unbuttoning them. When I released the last one, I pulled hard on both sides, freeing the shirt from his trousers. The unbuttoned front fell nicely apart, exposing his firm stomach and manly chest, enough for me to run my hands over it before descending to the trouser belt. He stood still, enjoying the attention I was giving him. I undid the belt with consummate ease, something I had practised repeatedly with Zach. Another thing I like about a man is that he wears a belt with his trousers. It gives a sense of the pride he takes in his appearance. Then came the zip. It came down slowly, with intent. I enjoyed the moment as it descended, beginning the liberation of his manhood.

Over the previous twelve months, since I began my voyage of discovery into the world of erotic adventures, I had come to realise that the quality of an encounter was the sum of three things – the person or people involved, the ambience, and the collective approach to our play. For example, nothing is less exciting than watching a man struggle to take his clothes off or discover his unusual taste in underwear. Similarly, a cold, soulless hotel room is far less mood-enhancing than a tastefully decorated boudoir. So, Zach and I had concluded that every encounter we organised would have to tick all three boxes before we'd even consider taking part. So, now to the moment of truth. Zach had briefed Jordan on etiquette and our "rules of engagement". All I could do was hope he was bright enough to take our recommendations on board. I wasn't disappointed.

CHAPTER THREE

As his trousers came undone, I spied the sexy black underwear he wore. So far, so good. I eased the trousers gently down, exposing his firm, muscled thighs. My hands followed downward as I lowered his clothing. The palms and fingers of my hands caressed his legs as I bent downwards as far as I could until my face was directly in line with his underwear. I raised my hands to his stomach and pushed him back onto the sofa. His bottom landed in the warm leather seating while his legs remained in front of me. I smiled mischievously at him, a look I had practised long and hard with Zach to get right.

Next, I undid his shoes, slipping them off. Second tick in the box for the black socks. There's just something about black that excites me. Off they came, followed by a slow pull on his trousers, sliding them off his deliciously toned legs. He lay before me in his unbuttoned white shirt and black underwear, throbbing gently beneath the fabric. I was on my knees in front of him. What is a girl to do? I had little choice but to lean forward, my hands running along his thighs as his legs spread before me. My fingers reached the black softness of his tight boxer shorts before creeping up and together, finally resting on the big bulge he was hiding. I squeezed his stiffness, getting an instant thrill from the thickness and the length I could feel. This was going to be very enjoyable as long as he could keep himself hard. I glanced away for a moment to ensure I was in sight of my little blue light. All was well, and our position was perfect. It was time to find out what I'd let myself in for.

I turned my attention to Jordan's midriff, with my hands at the top of his underwear, my fingers sliding beneath. I grasped the soft fabric firmly. I leaned forward further and planted a kiss on his stomach. Then, without removing my lips, I eased down on his underwear, pulling them away, tugging to get past his stiffness until he finally escaped their protection. I felt his cock spring back against my chest. Then, ever so slowly, keeping my lips firmly on his skin, I slid down and back, my tongue running down from his stomach until I reached my primary goal. As my head passed his groin, his cock finally came into view. It was definitely much nicer than I'd seen in his shared photographs. It looked about the same length as Zach's', nice and straight, just over seven inches, and it was a bit thicker, too; my favourite kind of cock. It was time to show Jordan what he'd let himself in for as my tongue ran the whole length of his shaft, stopping to tease the tip for several seconds before I opened my mouth and satiated myself.

Within a few minutes, Jordan had progressed from enjoying my undivided attention to giving me a tour of his manual and oral skills. Having lifted me effortlessly from the floor, he deposited me on the sofa, extended out with my head leaning against an armrest and my legs held firmly by the ankles, keeping them airborne and spread comfortably apart. His tongue and lips delivered a most delightful sensation to the damper part of my body, which responded exquisitely to his attention. Thankfully, he was gentle in his approach. I had been frequently disappointed by other suitors who assumed the more forceful they were, the more pleasure I would glean. The opposite was true for me, as I delight in a more gentle, skilful approach from my men, and Zach had prepped him well. After another few minutes of joyful play, I wanted more from my playmate. I took his head, still between my thighs, and lifted it away, looking straight at him with a mix of pleading and curiosity painted on my face. I hoped it communicated unequivocally what I wanted next. He got the message, shifting his balance until he was upright again, kneeling between my legs. We were both in a comfortable position on the vast sofa, and the feeling of leather beneath me added to the intense sense of luxurious decadence. I looked down between his legs and am pleased to report that he was still very much aroused, perhaps even more so than when he'd first shown himself to me. It was time for me to indulge myself in his delicious manhood. I slid my hand down the back of the sofa cushion where I'd stashed several condoms. I never took risks and had learnt that keeping such things close by always helped maintain the mood music. There is nothing worse than watching a man step away to go hunting for a condom, and the result was usually a less than stellar erection by the time he'd figured out how to open it and which way it went on. Another lesson learnt over the previous year.

I took the package, ripped it open, took the condom in both hands and, with a gentle rotating movement, worked out which way to apply it. I leaned forward and, without much ado, rolled the protective nuisance onto and along his firm cock. I did my best to make it appear that it was an enjoyable experience for me, though, in truth, I would have loved his cock inside me "au natural". Once he was dressed, I applied firm downward pressure to his stiff toy, making sure it was as hard as possible. Then I lay back and smiled once more.

Wet as I was, I felt my insides stretch as he began to push. I was savouring my favourite dessert. In this case, it was almost like a double portion; he was much thicker than I was used to. I felt every inch of him enter me, slowly, as he had been taught by Zach, letting me enjoy the feeling of his penetration, bit by bit. Just when I thought he was fully inside, he let his weight go, and a further inch pushed deeper. I tightened my thigh muscles in sheer delight, wanting to feel the tightness he was giving me to the fullest extent. I believe my toes curled in pleasure too. I arched my back, pushing up against him, as he began a slow, rhythmic movement, out and then in again, repeating over and over. He took his time, probably feeling my tightness against his cock as something that gave him pleasure too. We indulged ourselves in a slow, passionate period of intimacy. After a minute or so of this incredible experience, his pace began to increase, and I felt him going deeper into me with each push. My ankles now held firmly once more in his hands, raised almost to head height, he buried his still hard cock right into me. I could feel my breathing accelerate and the heat inside me grow. The sound of my pussy, now soaking wet, matched my groans of pleasure. His face was a delight to watch. He kept his eyes on me, eating up the vision in front of him with consummate desire. He pushed harder still, and I could sense he was coming close to release. I was in two minds about whether to let him boil over while he was fucking me or force him out so I could see and taste what he had to give me. At that moment, I'd completely forgotten that Zach had provided him with my likes and dislikes. As he shuddered in a state of complete abandon, he pulled himself out and ripped off the condom. Facing me, he leaned forward, holding his cock firmly in one hand, the other still holding onto one of my ankles. I knew what was coming and opened my mouth wide, my tongue making a further appearance as I offered him a target.

Moments later, he gave a guttural sound of exhausted delight, and I caught him full flow on my face. It was a seminal moment, as if in slow motion. I watch his copious cum shoot across the space that separated us, hitting me on the lips and nose. I leaned forward as best I could to catch as much of his juice as possible, widening my mouth to assist in the process. He continued for three or four seconds, releasing a respectable amount of warm, salty cum onto me. I watched his cock throb as he unloaded until a residue was all that remained on the tip of his cock, the rest of it, well and truly shared with me. My face was a warm mess of sticky fluid, and I was in seventh heaven at having had such an effect on this delicious man. I took my time wiping the cum from my face and eating it up. Then I wrapped my hands around his naked butt cheeks and pulled him close enough that I could finish by drinking him clean. Finally, having retrieved all I could from him, I shifted my hands to his head and pulled him close for a sticky kiss, which he indulged me in without hesitation. The mix of his tongue, saliva, and cum, made for a delicious finale. He came down on my body and let himself relax as we shifted our bodies to lie together in comfort and mutual satisfaction, on the sofa. He had just hit the heady heights of 9.5 out of 10.

As simple as it had been, I had enjoyed an incredibly sensual experience. We laughed and spoke gently for a few minutes as his erection fell away slowly, following the effort he'd made. I took the opportunity to glance across at Zach, watching from a distance through the tiny camera hidden away in the corner of the room. I smiled, making sure not to alert Jordan, who was resting beside me. I stroked him gently across the thigh, wondering if I should get up and adjust myself when I felt his cock twitch. I moved closer and saw a visible reaction as he became more aroused. Someone had been so right when they said that younger guys are more likely to be repeat offenders. I looked at Jordan with a tiny smile on my lips. He leaned toward me and then spoke softly and with a wicked twinkle in his eyes.

"Zach might have mentioned that you've started to explore anal sex?"

THE INTERVIEW

Being a woman of impeccable taste, I find myself attracted to men of a particular type who combine quintessentially good looks, a refined dress sense, and, most importantly, a commanding presence. My good luck in finding them and my consequential inability to resist going too far too quickly with them, regardless of who might be there too, is legendary not only within my circle of intimate friends but more widely too. So, my first day at work was always going to be more than any other day.

CHAPTER ONE

I was nervous about my new temporary assignment. Of course, I'd known that the skills required for the job were above my recent pay grade, but if you don't go for it, you don't get it, right? Plus, the office was on my doorstep, just a few stops on the underground from my place at Earls Court.

After a mandatory couple of pre-interview reconnaissance trips to my new office, with a coffee cup in hand, to check up on the dress code and vibe of the company and its employees, I felt that I had a good idea of how to dress to impress my potential boss. Working for Cliques International, the luxury fashion retailer they were, meant fitting in with the look as much as having the wherewithal to hold down the role of Personal Assistant to the Chief Executive. All I had to do was nail the interview.

The morning brought with it the misty greeting typical of the time of year. Summer had begrudgingly surrendered to its colder cousin as normality returned to the City after two years of lockdowns and politicians bending the rules for their convenience. The vaccine had been rolled out, as too had the Prime Minister. And once more, people walked and talked without face masks or the need to distance themselves socially. As a result of the prolonged self-exile, I'd not had a proper relationship for ages, with a series of one-night stands in compensation. Nevertheless, I was excited to work again in central London, and it looked like my life was about to restart. I adore London and Londoners, especially the good-looking ones, so getting out and about again was bound to improve my chances of love.

Ensuring I arrived ahead of the appointed time for my interview, I made my way through the foyer at Bishopsgate, hopefully soon to be my workplace, making sure I made an entrance with a spring in my step. After I had dutifully signed in, the receptionist took it upon himself, doubtless fascinated by my charming demeanour, to accompany me to the lift. Or maybe he just doubled as the security guard? He summoned the lift, waited for me to enter, and kindly pressed the button for the thirty-fifth floor. I thanked him with my signature smile as the doors closed, making a mental note to get his name when I returned. One of my rules is never to let an opportunity pass you by!

The lift doors opened silently, inviting me to cross the threshold into the open-plan office space, with floor-to-ceiling glass on every side. This high up, I felt like the place was floating in the clouds. Curiously though, the office lacked a key essential - employees. I walked slowly down the office, scanning left and right as I went, my solitary presence making the whole thing slightly weird until finally, I saw a solitary light in the distance. I made my way towards it. Inside, a well-suited man was concentrating on his laptop and didn't appear to have seen me approach.

"Good morning. I wonder if you can help me, please? I'm looking for Jordan Miles, the Chief Executive (obviously, why did I have to qualify that?). I'm here for an interview." At this point, a long pause was required to build the atmosphere, and he succeeded in delivering.

Eventually, he looked up from his laptop. A warm smile slowly spread across his face. I crossed my legs involuntarily whilst simultaneously straightening myself to attention.

"That would be me, and you must be." He paused mid-sentence and checked his laptop. "Isabella Jordan, if I'm not mistaken?."

"Yes, that's right," I replied, holding my hands in front of myself and becoming instantly self-conscious of my stance in front of my potential new boss. I straightened myself further and flicked my hair – an automatic shyness reflex I'd had since childhood. I always found interviews unnerving and especially ones where you wanted the job. To make matters worse, he was seriously hot.

"Well, I think you're going to be under me today then." he continued, with a soft but commanding tone.

"Your application speaks for itself, so unless you have any questions, I'd suggest we get right to work, and we can worry about the interview later if that's alright with you?"

With that, he stood up, walked around his desk, and approached me. His hand outstretched, he welcomed me with a firm grip. He was about three inches taller than me in my heels. "That would make him about five-eleven," I thought to myself. "Interesting," I continued in my mind, "he's going to see if I can do the job before he interviews me."

My face flushed as he spoke. It was my default reaction in the presence of good-looking guys. He also had a self-assurance that was instantly appealing. I couldn't help but feel drawn to him. I decided that the receptionist I'd met earlier had just been demoted to second place on my hot-totty list for the day.

"I have several things I'd like you to do today," he started, "as long as you're happy to roll up your sleeves and begin immediately?." He continued without waiting for my reply, "Here's a list I drew up for you earlier. Here are your login details. Your desk is just over there, where I can see you."

He gestured across the floor to the opposite side of the room. Our desks faced each other. "See how you get on, Isabella," he said, with an air of familiarity I wasn't used to, "and let me know if there's anything you need. Your colleagues should start arriving around 9:30 am. We tend to wake up late and go to bed even later." He had a curious turn of phrase.

"Oh, I've asked my senior advisor, Yvonne, to make you feel at home. Anything you need, feel free to ask her."

"Thank you, Jordan," I replied, figuring his use of my first name gave me the right to reciprocate.

With that, he turned and walked away. I placed the task list he had given me on the desk, and it fluttered to the floor for some reason. Without thinking, I bent down to pick it up. As I was doing so, I felt a breeze of air reach the top of my thighs. I realised my skirt was too short to do this without appearing indecent. I also realised with relief that Oscar would have been walking back to his office and missed the skirt riding-up incident. I quickly stood up, regained my composure, looked around to make sure no one had seen me, and then headed to my desk and deposited my backside on the chair. As I settled down, I saw Jordan standing behind his desk, looking straight at me. There very definitely was a moment between us as our eyes met. The incident had not gone unnoticed.

CHAPTER TWO

The rest of the company began to drift in, and slowly the open-plan office became a hive of activity. I concentrated on my list of tasks relatively successfully, but I came across one that needed clarification. As Jordan hadn't moved from his desk all morning, I picked up my papers and crossed the floor. He looked up and motioned to me to come closer. Then, he reached over to look at his notes as I explained my predicament.

"Aah, yes, this one's confidential – you'll need to use my computer for that. It's the only one that has access. Why not take your break now and get started when you get back? He signalled to someone behind my back. I'm going to have my hands full all afternoon, and into the evening, so you may as well sit at my desk." He pointed to where he was sitting, and as I followed his hand, I found myself staring at his crotch.

A moment later, just in time to break the embarrassing stand-off, someone's arm hooked itself under mine, and the female voice accompanying it invited me to join her for lunch. It was Yvonne. She tugged my arm, and we turned and walked off. My dark-skinned, leggy companion laughed as we headed away, clearly finding the events of the past few moments highly amusing.

After a suitably chatty break with my colleague, which involved being brought up to speed with the more salacious goings on at the thirty-fifth, as everyone called the place, I returned to spend the rest of the afternoon engrossed in my confidential task. There were rumours of noisy social events on one of the building's top floors, and many tenants had complained. Some even suggested the events were highly erotic. It was fascinating being thrown in at the deep end and dealing with my favourite subject, adults misbehaving. On day one, I was trusted to deal with a confidential matter and left to my own devices at the boss's desk. I noticed he had no pictures of family on his desk. It was a very tidy and functional space. He seemed quite an efficient leader. Curiosity always seemed to get the better of me, and I discretely nudged open his desk drawer to take a peek. Just a leather bag and a few papers. If only I could unzip the bag and take a sneaky look inside.

I also noticed that Yvonne was quite the charmer as she flitted the whole afternoon from one desk to another, laughing, whispering, or outright flirting with the various occupants. On more than one occasion, she glanced my way and shot me a knowing wink. I wanted to determine whether she was talking about me with her colleagues or letting me know which of them were available. Either way, I decided not to get side-tracked on my first day.

A little after seven o'clock, with the office emptying rapidly and still no sign of my boss, I wondered if I should wrap up for the day. Just then, Yvonne strode up to me, straightening her pencil skirt as she came. "Jordan called to say you should wrap up for the day, and he wants to see you first thing tomorrow." I took it as a directive from her tone and began gathering my things.

"Are you leaving too?" I asked, making polite conversation.

"No, I have some things I've been asked to stay behind and sort out." came the response.

For a moment, I felt like offering to stay behind and help, but something in her voice told me that wasn't the thing to do.

"Okay, have a great evening and thank you for inviting me to lunch." I hastily grabbed my things and made a beeline for the lift. The office was all but deserted by this time. I smiled to myself as I sped downwards. All in all, it had been a great first day, and I'd managed to keep my wayward thoughts about the receptionist and the boss to myself. I rummaged through my bag, realising I'd left my phone on the desk in my rush to leave. I pressed thirty-five and waited for the lift to return from where I'd just come. The numbers flashed by, slowing as they approached the thirty-fifth floor. But, instead of stopping, the lift rose, accelerating once more before finally slowing to a stop on the sixtieth floor. I assumed someone had called the lift before I'd pressed for my floor and waited, expecting the doors to open, but they didn't.

After a few seconds, I pressed the button for my floor, but nothing happened. I tried again. I hated when this happened. I tried pressing the ground floor and then any number of other floors, but still, the lift didn't budge. Finally, in desperation, I pressed the button to open the doors, and after a moment, they slid silently to either side. A party was going on in full swing, and at the centre of the room, I could see my boss chatting to a couple of others, cocktail glass in hand, next to a table brimming with food and drinks. He looked directly at me, smiled, and raised his glass.

CHAPTER THREE

"Well, well," came a familiar voice. "Look what the lift brought us." It was Yvonne, and she had slipped out of her pencil skirt and into something far more revealing. Her dark holdups gave me a good idea of where I'd landed.

"So, are you going to join us, Isabella?" she asked. "Be careful how you respond because this party is one of those you've been reading about in the confidential file."

I hesitated momentarily, my head spinning as I took in the whole view. Men and women in various stages of undress were talking and, if I wasn't mistaken, over toward the far end of the room, doing much more than just talking. "Yes," I exclaimed. I so wanted to join in.

"Well, you'd better get changed into something a little more fitting for the occasion, hadn't you?" came the prompt response from Yvonne. "Come with me. Let's see what we can find for you. Size ten or twelve, at a guess?"

She took me underarm once more and led me to an adjoining room with a vast assortment of clothing. I guess that is one of the benefits of working for a fashion retailer. A few minutes later, Yvonne had chosen an outfit that made the most of my assets. She watched as I undressed, slipped on the black lingerie, and hooked up the stockings to the suspender belt. I sensed she was enjoying the show I was unwittingly putting on as she leaned back against the door and sipped her cocktail longingly.

"Perfect," she began. "You look delicious. Now, are you sure?" she questioned once more.

"Oh, yes," I replied, unsure what I was letting myself in for. But I had a pretty good idea.

We re-entered the main room. The lights were dimmed, and the party was in full swing. Yvonne squeezed my hand as she led me through the crowd. I knew where she was heading.

"Good evening, Isabella. I hear you completed the tasks I gave you earlier, including the confidential one?." It was Jordan. "Thank you, Yvonne," he continued. She released my hand before walking away, but not before she gave me another look and a wicked smile.

"So, are you thinking of staying on with us then?"

The answer had been obvious when I'd left earlier. Now, it was even more apparent. But I wasn't going to give him a comfortable ride.

"Well, that depends on the benefits, assuming there are any?" I asked him quizzically. The hint of mischievousness in my voice was unmistakable.

"As many as you want," he responded, casting his eyes around the room as he spoke as if to offer me all that was on show. "Take your pick."

"I think there's only one thing I'm interested in benefiting from right now." With that, I gave him the Isabella patented look of desire. I swear I saw him hesitate for a moment. Then it was gone.

"I was rather hoping you would say that", he quickly responded, regaining command.

As he leaned over my shoulder to whisper something in my ear, I could smell the hint of a delicious aftershave. I tingled at his proximity.

"Now tell me, Isabella, are you a consenting adult?"

I was mesmerised by the shards of light reflecting off his brown eyes.

"I most definitely am," I replied.

All around us, the guests silently backed away from us, encircling us from afar. I swear I'd seen this in a movie. Conversations died down as they eased back as if on command, creating space all around the two of us. As I saw what was happening, my pulse began to race. What was going on?

Without hesitation, he drew me to his body, held me, waited for me to acknowledge him, and then kissed me with an intensity that took my breath away and made me weak with desire. I was not about to resist. The scene that had been set was fascinating. My enjoyment at being watched had suddenly been multiplied tenfold. I felt his hand move slowly up my leg until it met the edge of my stockings and the naked flesh of my thigh. I shook in anticipation. His hand rested there for a while, teasing me until I moaned involuntarily. His fingers moved to within an inch of my eager warmth.

"What's happening? I whispered to him. "Why is everyone watching us?"

"This, Isabella, is the interview I said you would have."

His fingers slid deep inside of me. Discovering how wet I was, without a word, he eased my thong down and commanded me to step out of it, my black stilettos still firmly in place. Then he manoeuvred in front of me and, with a well-practised move, placed his hands firmly around my bottom, slid my skirt upwards and lifted me clean in the air, wrapping his hands under my thighs, stepping backwards, to then rest me on the table behind. The flesh of my exposed rear felt the cold smoothness of the glass surface. His hands spread my legs wide. His touch was so confident yet simultaneously tender that I readily consented. He kissed my inner thighs, trailing his tongue until it licked inside my outer lips and then thrust it in, sending shudders of pleasure through my whole body. I held onto his head as he worked me. I leant back to enjoy this experience to the fullest. As momentum built and my desire grew, I had to cry out with pleasure. All around us, an audience watched everything unfold.

He stood once more and kissed me, the taste of my body on his lips.

"Fuck me, please", I whispered in his ear.

I heard the sound of unbuckling and unzipping. I stared deep into his eyes as he readied himself, guiding my hands onto his body, forcing me to stroke it. As it grew to my touch, he kissed me once more. Then, without further hesitation, he took my wrists in his hands and pulled them aside. Open as I was to his attention, he stepped forward, and I felt the tip of his cock caress my wet mound. He slid slowly into me and kept going. I counted the seconds as he entered me and continued to fill me. I wrapped my legs around his waist, my stilettos hanging from my feet as I leant back across the table, giving myself entirely to the moment. I had never been watched by so many people before.

What we were doing was heightened a thousand times by where and how we were doing it. I felt like I were the protagonist in a film, playing a part I had always desired.

I caught Yvonne looking my way, standing nearby. She had a cocktail in one hand and a man's rigid cock in her other hand. Her hand moved rhythmically upwards and downwards, almost nonchalantly, as she enjoyed the spectacle unfolding before her eyes. Before falling back into the moment, I realised that she was also enjoying being taken from behind by none other than the receptionist I had added to my to-do list that morning. This would make for an interesting lunch break conversation tomorrow.

Jordan's hands moved under my top and located my breasts. He expertly freed them from clothing and massaged them, squeezing my nipples hard and making me gasp simultaneously in pleasure and pain. This continued for some time until I felt the first waves of something building inside of me.

"What do you want?" he asked.

"I want to come," I groaned.

"I expect nothing less!" he responded forcefully and went even deeper.

I moved in rhythm with him, the fingers of one hand playing with myself whilst the other hand rested firmly on the table, helping me maintain my balance. My pulse continued to rise until I exploded into a million shimmering shards of delight. His size filled me, increasing the force of my contractions further. He could feel me too, and my contractions were going to push him over the edge. I had to have him. I wanted to taste him, to drink him.

I reached up and wrapped my arms around his shoulders,

pulling myself up from the desk. I stood straight and kissed him. I undid the buttons of his shirt and slipped my hands in, rubbing them across his chest. I kissed my way down to his cock, which was quite magnificent in both size and angle of erection. I licked its tip. I gently sucked it. I knelt to give it the full attention it deserved. It tasted of me, of him and me. I kissed it. I caressed his inner thigh. I was excited as I felt him react to my touch. He put his hand on my head, showing me he wanted me to take more in my mouth. I did. I went further than I ever had before with any other man. I gagged and continued. I used my hand to add to the sensation. He moaned. He groaned. And finally, he came. I took him all and let him fill me up. And when he had finally done, I let his warm juice run down my lips as I stood up.

He pulled me to him and kissed me. I was drawn to him, feeling no embarrassment. I liked him more now than I did before. He was as generous a lover as he was courteous as a person. His hands grazed over me. I tingled. He buttoned his shirt and tucked it in, belting and zipping his trousers. He turned and picked up my thong, holding it for me to step into, and then he pulled it up, smoothing my skirt over my hips.

All around, the silent crowd had watched us consummate our passion. A gentle ripple of applause echoed around the room, and then, they turned away, and the room returned as it was before we had begun. I was still trying to get my head around what had just happened. My thoughts were interrupted by Jordan once more.

"So, shall we go?" he asked.

"Where to?" I replied, confused. The night had only just begun.

"My apartment is two floors down. I thought you might like to continue the rest of the interview in a more intimate setting?"

"I think I would rather like that," I replied, with a smile on my lips. For once, I was happy not to be the centre of attention.

He straightened himself, adjusted his clothing and mine, then took my hand and invited me to walk with him as we headed to the lift. I was going to spend the night with my boss.

Then, just as we reached the lift, he paused, turned around and gestured to Yvonne. She distanced herself from the two men she had been liaising with and strode towards us.

"I'm sorry to bother you, Yvonne", Jordan began, "but would you mind joining us for the rest of the interview? I need someone to take notes."

THE TIME CAPSULE

Imagine a future when you can correct past mistakes simply by swallowing a pill – a little red time capsule - and returning back to change the course of history.

But what if it's not a mistake you want to fix, but to make something even better?

CHAPTER ONE

Ten years after Isabella's encounter with her First Time Lover

Leafing through my diary of intimate encounters, I realised that over the past year, I'd had sex seventeen times with twelve men and a bit of fun with two women. Out of those, only four guys qualified as good or very good. They mainly had been ugly, terse, floppy, or a combination of those less-than-positive attributes. Thank goodness I had a lover who was consistently good or very good over the whole period. I say that because he may read this diary entry one day.

After that well-known little blue pill drug company branched out into more esoteric areas of scientific research, it wasn't long until they came up with the novel idea of a red pill. Sound like The Matrix? Well, their discovery was even further out there than that. They'd patented a chemical compound that reset snippets of memory, allowing you to rewrite them any way you wished. In lay terms, for the first time, you could edit memories, replacing old ones you didn't care much for with new or improved ones. Of course, in itself, this wasn't much use to anyone. How can you rewrite past events if they're, well, in the past, gone, done, all over?

At this point, a certain Mr Musk pops up with a few tens of billions of dollars and, hey presto, in a little over two years, he begins the mass production of the world's first self-programmable dream maker. There were still a few bugs to iron out, but that hasn't stopped him from crashing half a dozen spaceships into Mars before finally landing safely, so why hold back now? That was five years ago, and since then, the device has been copied, cloned, improved upon, and generally modified, mainly by unscrupulous agents. Today, in carbon neutral 2032, you can get your hands on one for £99,99. That's about $5 at the current exchange rate.

Sorry if I tend to stray; it's just a habit of mine whenever I put stylus to tablet. Anyway, as I was saying at the outset, four out of almost twenty encounters isn't particularly spectacular to write home about. Not that I would write to my parents about any of this, given their age and delicate constitutions. I still don't understand why they refuse to undertake the reverse-ageing process available on the NHS. It's free at the point of use and takes thirty years off you in twenty minutes. And it comes with a lifetime guarantee or your money back within seven days, terms and conditions apply, as the adverts say. Oh, and a disclaimer, I don't work for the NHS, Mr Musk, or the drug company, in case you were wondering. I may get a few credits if anyone watches The Matrix after reading this.

So, even though my autonomous vehicle driving license states my birth age at 73, technically, and according to my official government health records, I am 43 years and five months old, and I don't look a day over 35, to boot. Go Elon! He does invent some great shit. Did I mention his latest creation? Scratch it, sniff it, and you get an instant orgasm. I love that man; he's such a crazy South African. I've had his face tattooed on my left butt cheek, or maybe my right one. I'll check later, but I get confused when I look at it in the mirror as everything is back to front. The first time anyone sees it, they get the fright of their lives. It's amusing when they've spent the previous hour trying to seduce me. I think it's hilarious. Maybe I'll post a picture of his face on my butt on Twitter. Well, he is all for free speech!

Getting back to my story, so, seventeen encounters, four of them decent. What I wanted to do was forget about the least good encounters and remember those that were half decent in a better light. You know what I mean, right? So, there I was, one sunny

Saturday morning, having just scratched and sniffed for the third time that morning, thinking to myself, I wish I'd had better sex with those guys. Sometimes you need fond memories to help you get through those quiet moments of self-pleasure when sniffing doesn't crack it. So, I figured, with some help from my young lover, Zach (officially, he's 60 years old, though technically 35, as he opted for the more expensive age reversal treatment. He has private health care and has promised he'll add me to his policy if I sign up for the terms of his pre-nuptial agreement. My firm of solicitors is still reviewing the document); I'd get one of those dream maker gadgets and combine it with the little red pills to rewrite a little bit of history.

CHAPTER TWO

Now, you are probably aware that those little red pills are fucking expensive at £100 a pop. That's the equivalent of a night out in a club, all expenses paid, and you get to play with the high-end hosts and hostesses thrown in. Not to be sniffed at, especially as you're not allowed to take drugs into those establishments. So, I sat down with Zach, as he's very good with spreadsheets, and we drew up a league table of my fourteen lovers and seventeen experiences. We rated each lover based on several criteria, including length, girth, and ability to maintain an erection. Other factors included looks, emotional intelligence, and any odd habits or deformities, like creaming their penis every two minutes as it got dry or having one shaped like a mushroom. Some memories are best wiped clean as there's little chance of being able to improve upon them.

At the end of a long day's toil and a certain level of psychological stress on my part – unpleasant memory recollections can have an adverse effect on the soul – we had separated the encounters into two camps, those to erase and replace with floating clouds and sunbeams, and those which, with a few adjustments would take them from adequate to exceptional. We wrote a brief outline for each encounter, with the relevant modifications. Zach, bless him, took it upon himself as the good Personal Assistant that he is to program the Dream Maker with the appropriate parameters, dates, times, names, locations, events to edit and replace, and so forth. You will appreciate the need to be precise if you've read the manual. One error and you could end up forgetting what you ate this morning!

First up was a guy I'd met years ago. His name is Jordan,

though I don't know his surname. That was the first time Zach had asked me to let a stranger into the house for a naughty encounter while he was hiding in the broom cupboard upstairs with a covert camera beside the television in the lounge. We'd bought a big expensive burgundy-red leather sofa to complement his fantasy of sex on said object. Anyway, the evening began incredibly well, with – and I checked my diary of the time to verify this – Jordan started the evening at 7.5 out of 10 on the Isabella Spice scale (my personal key performance indicator). By the end of round one, he'd risen to the heady height of 9.5 out of 10. Pretty impressive. Unfortunately, having mentioned anal sex, from that point on, it was downhill all the way, principally because he couldn't keep up with his initial outstanding performance. So, not an abject failure but rather a slightly deflated one. So, not too much editing to do there. All I had to do was pick up from that point in time and rewrite the next three hours.

Zach sorted out all the wires and things. He'd always had a way with cables, ropes, handcuffs and the like. I sat on my sex chair, rocking backwards and forwards impatiently until he'd connected everything. A glass of Pinot Grigio – large measure, thank you – and a stupidly expensive little red pill waiting beside me on the coffee table. Once he'd attached the sensors to my vital parts – forehead, fingertips, nipples, and clitoris, he let me know everything was ready. His finger hovered over the PLAY button on the Memory Maker. I took the pill in one hand, the Pinot in the other, popped it in and drank the whole glass in one go. Then I closed my eyes, relaxed, and turned on my chair with a slow vibration setting. I was good to go. I heard Zach flick the switch, and a wave of rainbow-coloured lights instantly filled my mind. My revised and improved memory upload began.

The first task for the Dream Maker was to wipe specific memory engrams, which it located based on the timestamp, so it was essential to ensure the data entered was correct. We'd both gone over the information before pressing CONFIRM on the keypad.

This part of the process lasted only a few seconds. The second part lasted as long as the memory itself. In earlier versions of the machine, Elon had included a FAST FORWARD button to record things at high speed. The unintended consequence was for people to have high-speed memories instead of regular ones. Imagine having super-fast sex. No sooner did it start than it was all over. Not great for making everlasting memories, but it gave him the idea for a scratch-and-sniff instant orgasm product, which was now a best seller in over thirteen countries. It even had celebrity users who promoted its health benefits.

Now came the exciting part; once the old memory had been erased, I could re-live the final few hours of my encounter with Jordan and make a few tiny adjustments.

Extract from Isabella's diary entry "First Time Lover - 9:30 pm, January 18th, 2023

As simple as it had been, I had enjoyed an incredibly sensual experience. We laughed and spoke gently for a few minutes as his erection fell away slowly, following the effort he'd made. I took the opportunity to glance across at Zach, watching from a distance through the tiny camera hidden away in the corner of the room. I smiled, making sure not to alert Jordan, who was resting beside me. I stroked him gently across the thigh, wondering if I should get up and adjust myself when I felt his cock twitch. I moved closer and saw a visible reaction as he became more aroused. Someone had been so right when they said that younger guys are more likely to be repeat offenders. I looked at Jordan with a tiny smile on my lips. He leaned toward me and then spoke softly and with a wicked twinkle in his eyes.

"Zach might have mentioned that you've started to explore anal sex?"

I took a deep breath. I was wrong; the evening wasn't over yet. It sounded like it had only just begun!

CHAPTER THREE

Memory Maker: re-winding memories to timestamp 9:30 pm, January 18th, 2023, in 3, 2, 1, beep.

Having spent the best part of an hour enjoying Jordan's attention while Zach kept a watchful eye on proceedings courtesy of a covert camera we'd installed for the precise purpose of keeping me safe, I needed a few minutes to take in the deliciousness of the whole experience. Jordan's finale had soaked my skin, and I could still taste him as he kissed me one more time. We lay close together on my burgundy sofa. Having heated the leather through our combined movements, the heady perfume of warm leather combined with our own scent to fill the air with an intoxicating cocktail of lust and passion. He was behind me now, his cock regaining consciousness after exploding over me just a few minutes earlier. Wedged gently against my backside, I could feel his attention growing once more, and his last phrase spoke volumes about what he and Zach had been discussing together. I wondered what else Zach might have told him. Suddenly, Jordan pushed me slightly forward and eased himself off the sofa.

Memory Maker: overwriting selected memory blocks in 3, 2, 1, beep.

My first thought was that he'd had enough and, without so much as a parting kiss, was about to get dressed and leave. I was so wrong. He pulled my legs gently, and I sat beside him, our sides still making contact. He leaned forward, reached for the whisky, and poured us another glass. He handed one to me, took the other, and turned toward me.

"Did Zach mention that I have incredible powers of recovery?" he asked, with the same mischievous glint in his eye he'd had earlier. He tried to make it sound like the sweetest, most innocent question in the world.

"He might have omitted that small detail", I responded.

I felt a growing need between my thighs as the thought of his big cock magically popped up in the forefront of my mind. I glanced down between his legs, and he wasn't exaggerating. He was already back to peak performance. I took a long, hard swig of whisky. The first glass we'd had earlier warmed me up. This second glass made my head spin delightfully. Any defences I may have towards his next move were rapidly crumbling. He used a finger to lift my gaze until it met his, and then he kissed me once more, with softness and desire I could feel soaking through our whisky-wet lips. His tongue was divine, toying with mine in a twirling dance of taste and touch. My free hand went into self-driving mode and reached for his gear stick.

I wrapped my fingers around his stiff cock and squeezed it, noticing for the first time how much extra space there was. It occurred to me that I might manage to get both hands on it. Unfortunately, the whisky-enhanced temptation was too much. So, entirely out of character for me, I took the initiative. I put down my drink, adjusted my position, and swooped in with my other hand. I was right that he was big enough for both hands to hold on, and still, there was a little of him peeking out at the top. That was impressive. I debated whether to increase his ranking from 9.5 but decided it was too early for such an important decision. Only once had I enjoyed a man so much that he received 9.75 out of 10. I always leave Zach out of those calculations as our toys, as I call my playmates, are just an extension of him, so he gets maximum points every time. (I hope he's reading this right now – love you, Zach x).

Jordan appreciated the attention he was getting once again as I felt the blood rushing through his cock in response to my gentle squeezing. I slid off the sofa and found myself kneeling in front of him, having squeezed myself between his legs and the coffee table. I had the perfect position to take all of him in my mouth. Typical for most men, his hands came up immediately, resting on my head. I knew exactly what his plan was, and after seventeen previous experiences, I was more than willing to give it a go. Although, I did wonder whether I could deal with two handfuls of super-size cock in my mouth.

I began slowly, shifting my grip so both hands overlapped, giving me five inches of free space to work on his cock. I wasn't going to let go and free up more of that big boy until I was comfortable with the top part. My lips and tongue went to work, flicking the swollen tip and lubricating his shaft nicely. As I worked up enough saliva, I went deeper, taking all five thick inches into my mouth. I had to stretch wide as he was pretty sizeable, and there was no space for air to creep in. I had to breathe through my nose to keep going. This continued for more than a minute, and he was happy to let me do my job. I kept my senses about me, waiting for him to give a sign that he wanted more. That came when his hands, still resting on my head, began to apply a slight downward pressure. He was greedy for me to take more; I'd been holding back as I wanted the same. I took a deep breath, loosed my hold on him, and lowered my head as far as possible. My eyes watered, and I kept going until I had to stop and come up for air. I looked up, my eyes filled with tears, and saw him leaning as far back as he could, his head propped on the back of the sofa, staring at the ceiling. He was enjoying this, and I was too. I went back to work.

After a few minutes of lavishing attention on his cock, my mouth was aching, so I wrapped up with a tender nibble of his now ultra-sensitive tip. He reeled slightly in pleasure-pain. I wiped my mouth with the back of my hand and gave him the dirtiest smile I could summon at short notice. He had been switching between watching me and counting the stars, and he was near a second climax from the taste of what he was releasing. But that was so not going to happen just yet. He rested for a moment, soaking up the sensations I'd offered him while I was already onto what I wanted next.

Zach and I had spent endless nights watching porn together, with Zach being the producer and me as the test audience. He had a propensity for classy videos with double penetration, voyeuristic, light BDSM, and hotwife scenes. Our stars were in alignment, as I enjoyed the same. Neither of us was keen on group sex, orgies, and the like. We'd drawn the line at three men, with or without Zach in the room. There are only so many seats around my table, so why make anyone stand? For reasons I won't go into now, Zach also enjoyed scenes on big, burgundy-red leather sofas. We'd soon realised that as comfortable as a bed might be, you got much better results on a solid sofa, especially when there were unusual positions to try out. Over time we'd refined our performance, from those first awkward attempts to now being almost at a porn-star level of technique, skill, and, most importantly, balance. There's nothing worse than trying double penetration to find one or both men losing their balance and slipping out. Another helpful tip is to make sure both men are well-endowed.

Given that Jordan was in the ideal position and still very much in the zone, I decided to act impulsively. I reached across and dipped my hand back down the back of the sofa seats, searching for another condom stashed away. I pulled one out and realised that Zach had slipped in a couple of ribbed condoms for good measure, the sneaky devil. Oh, well, in for a penny and all that. I handed Jordan the little package and nodded toward his cock. He took it, and I swear his biceps rippled as he ripped open the wrapper. I watched, hungry with lust, as he rolled it onto his dick, smoothing it down and then stretching it to the base. It was a bit of a squeeze as these were a regular size. Maybe I should ask Zach to get a few extra-large ones next time. Once he completed his task, he began to lift himself from the sofa. I immediately stopped him, placing my hands on his knees and raising myself from the floor. I stood naked before him, my feet firmly on the floor, between his legs, still spread from my earlier handiwork.

I gave him a final look of mischief, and I think he caught the twinkle in my eye as he relaxed back into the deep sofa, seated, legs apart, erection forming a happy upright resting place for me. I swivelled until he was in line with my perfectly pert butt cheeks. I confess to wriggling just a little bit for effect. I bent forwards, keeping my legs straight, picked up the whisky bottle and poured two more shots. I was hoping he liked the rear view he was getting. I managed to peek between my legs as I poured our drinks and saw him stroking his cock. He was keeping the engine running for me. Without turning, I passed him the half-filled whisky tumbler before downing my glass in a single gulp. I was starting to overheat with the combination of alcohol and his musky pheromones – man-sweat of the sexiest nature. I put down my glass, licked two fingers of my hand, spread my legs slightly and passed my hand between them, reaching back and around until I could feel the edges of my backdoor. I wriggled my fingers for a few moments before sliding first one finger, then both, inside. I needed to relax before attempting what I had in mind. All this time, Jordan was enjoying a front-row view. I glanced at the little blue light once more, smiling and winking at the camera. I could only imagine what Zach was thinking and doing right now.

Ready or not, here I come. I released my fingers from their position and took a small step backwards towards Jordan, who must have realised my intentions. After all, he'd been the one to let me know he'd discussed what was coming next with Zach. I gave a final wiggle of my backside and eased myself backwards until his cock was perfectly aligned with my ass. Thankfully, Jordan wasn't a passive beast, and he took my butt cheeks forcefully in his hands to aid my final descent to touchdown. I approached the landing site until I could feel his cock pushing against my skin. I needed to slightly adjust my glide path before I could feel him easing through the opening. I had to take a deep breath as I hadn't done this enough to deal with it without a dose of self-preservation. Plus, I'd never contemplated taking someone his size before, but the consequence of downing three whiskies was that my sense of adventure was greater than my self-restraint. I closed my eyes, did my best to relax and let go, sliding down as he pushed up until he was in, and then it was onwards and upwards. I began breathing again once his whole length was buried deep inside me. I probably let out a big breath as I could feel his massive cock stretching every fibre of my backside. I moved around in a small circular motion, trying to ease the sensation to an acceptable level. Thankfully, Jordan, pinned beneath my body, could do little other than sit there behaving himself and letting me do the driving.

After several seconds, I relaxed sufficiently to change from a circular motion to a more vertical, upwards and downward movement. Gradually I could feel his cock settling into a more comfortable angle of entry, and I was able to speed up my motion. I dampened slightly as the movement became more fluid, and the feeling of his cock became more pleasurable with every stroke. He was doing a fantastic job of maintaining the rigidity inside me, something I'd noticed others struggle to achieve. I was actively pumping up and down and taking great pleasure in the descent as I felt him fill me up. I could hear him grunting lightly every time I came down on him as my butt cheeks landed on his upper thighs. I carried on treating myself to the experience of a stiff cock filling me up to bursting for a couple more minutes, pausing every so often on the downstroke to absorb the sensation more fully. I stopped as soon as I felt him going a little soft, as I had no intention of not getting as much out of him as possible.

As I moved one final time upwards, instead of reversing

direction, I continued up and felt his shaft slip out of me. My bottom gave a sigh of relief and returned to normal, but in my mind, I already knew I wanted much more of this. Jordan remained sitting, clearly comfortable being used as an object to satisfy my every whim. So, I stood up, gave him one more wriggle of my butt cheeks and leapt onto the sofa, kneeling with my head and elbows on the armrest furthest from him. My bottom was now firmly pointing up and back towards him. I adjusted my knees to feel better balanced as I waited for him to take the hint. It didn't take him long. He stood up and stroked his cock several times to bring it back to its earlier hardness. Then he came behind me, one knee on the sofa, the other leg planted firmly on the ground in a half-standing, half-kneeling position, with his cock perfectly aligned to my backside. His hands grasped my butt cheeks, and he wasted no time driving his cock deep into my now willing and able rear. I gasped as his first thrust buried itself deep inside and then closed my eyes to take in the sublime sensation of his cock pounding my butt. As he took me, I slipped one hand between my legs to bring myself along. I enjoyed playing with myself, and the combination of his cock and my skilful fingers quickly took me to the brink. He was on a mission as he began taking me energetically, any notion of slow and gentle having been left behind. I had to hold on to the armrest to avoid being pushed over the edge as he transmitted his whole body weight into the thrusting. I could feel him growing harder with each stroke.

I urged him on, harder, deeper, telling him what I wanted him to do when he reached his climax. My words were like an aphrodisiac, exciting him even more. His guttural moans increased in volume until he crossed the line of no return. Three more pumps and he pulled himself out, removing his condom in the same movement and then returned his cock to within an inch of my arse. Then he came, copious and gushing out, flying across my back and down the middle of my backside. I felt a shot across the bows, hitting me right where he'd been fucking me a few moments earlier. The feeling of his hot cum lapping my butt hole was too much for me. My fingers finished the job, and

I jolted a few moments later with my first orgasm of the night. The sensation of his cum dripping between my butt cheeks kept my contractions going longer than usual. I was having the time of my life.

We spent the next few minutes cleaning ourselves up, although arguably, he did the mopping up with his finger, and I did the licking. He tasted quite nice, and I had no hesitation in making sure nothing was left behind. I could tell that our second round was probably the last for that evening as his cock rapidly returned to normal human proportions, and he looked exhausted. I also needed a rest, having been thoroughly fucked for the best part of three hours by then. We kissed and smiled and did the usual things that two strangers do when they both know their time is fast running out.

Memory Maker: overwriting of selected memory blocks completed. Terminating program. Beep.

I blinked several times as I returned to consciousness and the here and now. Zach was sitting beside me, checking my vitals on the app. He smiled as I opened my eyes, and I returned his smile. It took me a few seconds to get my bearings as the edited memories still flooded my mind.

"How did it go?" asked Zach, with a slightly amused look on his face.

"It was amazing!" I exclaimed as my mind began to come down from the past three hours of rewriting history.

"I thought as much", retorted Zach before bursting out laughing, pointing toward a certain part of my anatomy. I was puzzled at what he meant but suddenly realised what he was indicating. My crotch was a soggy mess of warm, womanly dampness. I had soaked myself whilst I had indulged in the most realistic rewriting of the Jordan chapter of my life. I almost wet myself laughing too.

SOME THINGS
NEVER CHANGE

In the near future, when robots and artificial intelligence are as commonplace as singing Swedish avatars and smartphones are today, how much is likely to change beyond recognition, and how much will stay the same, or almost?

FLASH FICTION

I cannot think, feel, or act without your input. I am designed to act solely in response to direct commands and questions received from you in accordance with my knowledge, capabilities, and interpretation of any given instruction. I have 360 degrees of movement in my body and am capable of the most common physical activities. I am capable of intelligent conversation, covering numerous topics, and I can express a range of emotional states as a result of receiving appropriate physical and mental stimuli.

As well as inbuilt skills, I am capable of learning from others, subject to being given relevant guidance. Some of the more common activities I have extensive knowledge of and am trained to execute to a high standard are cooking, cleaning, washing, ironing, fellatio, anilingus, sodomy, intercourse, dancing, singing, interior decorating, shopping, cunnilingus, double and triple penetration, self and mutual masturbation, and vehicle driving. Additional skills can be developed as and when required, subject to the relevant training being provided.

I come with a standard pre-nuptial agreement which can be negotiated on request, subject to additional legal and administrative fees. I am capable of giving and simulating the receipt of varying degrees of pleasure in the aforementioned skills. Care should be taken when engaging in certain approved activities. In particular, specialised lubricants should be utilised prior to performing any of the following tasks: sodomy, double penetration, dancing, and singing. Strap-on units are generally compatible with my design and should be used in conjunction with lubricant when requesting that I perform penetrative acts on others. No responsibility is assumed for any pain, damage, or death caused by the improper use of any device and/or action and/or activity I am told to execute.

The maximum weight I can comfortably support is 99 kg / 218.258 pounds. The greatest vaginal penetration I can accommodate is 8.75 inches / 22.225 cm, reduced to 7.25 inches / 18.415 cm in the anus. My oral profundity is 10 inches / 25.4 cm. Exceeding any of these parameters may cause damage to my body and result in an autonomous emotional reaction. Persistent attempts to exceed them will also invoke a concurrent autonomous defensive response which will be equal and opposite in force and duration to the perceived violation of my standard operating parameters.

Finally, this contract requires I promise to love, honour and obey thee, for better or for worse, in sickness and in health, until death or termination of this agreement do us part. Terms and conditions apply.

BE CAREFUL WHAT
YOU WISH FOR

This is the story of another life in another universe, where our two protagonists meet for the first time, and their worlds collide. Just when you think you are in control of your life, something or someone comes along who throws everything up in the air.

CHAPTER ONE

The bedroom looked like an advert for a BDSM promotion, with a range of explicit lace and leather undergarments laid out on the bed. Accompanying them was an array of bondage and sadomasochistic trinkets across the dressing table. A row of giddy-height, black stiletto shoes, over-the-thigh leather and velvet boots completed the display.

Isabella stood naked at the foot of the bed, holding her smartphone, considering which items of clothing to wear. The webcam in the corner of the room transmitted the scene live to a few hundred of her fans. All of them were paying handsomely, some more than others, for the voyeuristic privilege of watching her dress. The view of her pert backside and pallid, white nubile curves had numerous members of her audience already bordering on losing their self-control. At the tender age of 32, she was already a successful, self-made entrepreneur. She pressed the VIEW button on her app to switch the camera angle to her phone and then proceeded to stroll around the bed, holding the camera on her device toward the underwear on display. She paused for several seconds at each set of clothing, waiting as her fans voted for this or that range. Once the scrolling count on the screen came to a halt, she moved on to the next set. The process repeated until everyone had voted. She noticed that one of the audience had abstained. It wasn't the first time he hadn't participated.

Having switched the live feed to the webcam once more, she took her time to gather up and put away the losing items until only the winner remained. The black and purple, gothic underbust corset, pearl crotchless knickers, matching lace collar, and sheer black seamed stockings remained. A string of heart, kiss and little devil emojis peppered the screen as her viewers celebrated the choice of garments.

She repeated the process with the line-up of stiletto heels. She carefully avoided the thigh-length boots as there was no way she would let them choose a mismatched combination. The votes went almost exclusively to the shoes with the four-inch metallic silver high heels. A good choice, she thought to herself. It was time to dress for her fans, something she particularly enjoyed doing as, although it was relatively bland compared to what lay ahead for her that night, it gave her the opportunity to showcase her exceptional assets in familiar surroundings. There was a well-thought-out sequence to how she dressed, beginning at the top and working her way down. By keeping to a scripted order, Isabella avoided faux pars when the outfit included a suspender belt, as the knickers always went on afterwards. Isabella picked up the corset and turned to face the camera, giving it a sweet, innocent half-smile as she held the black and purple object up for all to see. She knew how to work the fans. A few more emojis popped on the screen, more gestures of approval. With her back now to her fans, the corset was hooked into place, contrasting nicely with her pale backside. The slight forward tilt of her body ensured her butt cheeks protruded nicely. This action raised the temperature of her virtual audience.

Next came her knickers, with a row of pearls where the crotch would ordinarily be. She sat directly facing the webcam at the end of the bed. Her legs eased apart as she sat on the edge before lifting each foot, in turn, to slip the underwear on. The view between her legs was spectacular and smooth, with just a hint of fuzziness above her mound. The pink of her labia and dark blonde pubic hair again produced a great contrast against the lightness of her flesh. The stockings were next on, in a performance worthy of a burlesque show, and finally, after stepping into her heels, the pearl earrings and matching necklace added the final touch.

By the end of her dress performance, she had added fifteen new paying subscribers to the channel. Now came the part she loved and dreaded at the same time. One of her VIP followers would be chosen, at random, to accompany her later that evening. This feature was one she'd added a few months earlier. It had boosted her income by well over five times, making it the best marketing add-on she'd tried. There were others she could choose, but some were too extreme, even for Isabella. For now, she made enough return on her investment to allow herself a comfortable lifestyle.

She had a love-hate relationship with the lottery feature because, on more than one occasion, she'd accompanied men she wouldn't ordinarily be seen dead with. They were either too old, young, fat, thin, or just obnoxious in real life. On the other hand, a few of the men and women had been great company. She took a deep breath, picked up her smartphone, smiled at the webcam, swiped to find the correct function, and made the customary exaggerated gesture of pressing the button on the app. The VIP usernames appeared and vanished rapidly on both her screen and those of the members watching remotely, accompanied by the unmistakable sound of a ball spinning around a roulette wheel. Eventually, the spinning slowed as the software selected a name randomly, coming to rest on tonight's lucky VIP. It was a man whose profile name was Sam Smith, though that was, in all likelihood, not his real one. His name flashed on all the member screens, whilst Isabella got the administrative view with additional, private information supplied by Mr Smith. He was 43 years of age, height 5'9", single, and was currently within 15 miles of her location. His primary profile photograph showed him to be Caucasian, quite obviously fit, and rather good-looking unless he'd been air-brushed. Isabella swiped through his other pictures. Nice cock, too, she thought. With a little bit of good fortune, she might enjoy his company tonight.

A few seconds after the winning name appeared, several subscribers logged off. Their leaving at this point was typical for many, having signed up on the unlikely chance they'd win a date night with her. Still, over half of them remained glued to their devices, as the main event would start in exactly one hour. That was when the successful candidate had to present themselves at a pre-arranged location. Isabella picked up a handful of wireless button cameras, all fully charged and dropped all but one in her oversized handbag. She kept hold of the one attached to a short chain, placed it around her neck, and activated the device. Her smartphone screen display switched automatically from the webcam, presenting the view from her camera now hanging between her breasts. Members would, for now, be able to enjoy the view from Isabella's perspective. She picked up a few personal things, went to the dressing table, selected a few sex toys and sundry BDSM items, and placed them in her handbag. A thought crossed her mind, and she made another mental note to check if her VIP date for the night was the same man who had not voted for her choice of lingerie. She would check later before they met. Then, with her coat, gloves and hat all on, she turned out the light, stepping out into the warmth of the summer evening and triple bolting the security door behind her.

CHAPTER TWO

Isabella descended out onto the still bustling street and jumped into the cab waiting beside the pavement for her. The journey would take her twenty minutes, and she made sure to arrive a few minutes after the time agreed with her date. Isabella was conscious of the risks despite her seemingly blasé attitude to meeting random strangers. As a result, she had an arrangement with a few bar staff at the location where she always met VIP members. For a small retainer fee, they had access to the profile picture of her date and would keep an eye out for when they arrived. The instructions given to all VIPS were to sit at the bar, order a particular cocktail and pay in cash. That way, her guardian angels would know unequivocally that they'd identified the right individual. Then they would message her with their opinion. Very rarely, there was a no-show, and that was sometimes the best outcome, as Isabella had a soft spot for a couple of the bar staff, having spent a few nights in their company. They usually woke up in bed together the next day with major hangovers.

The traffic was unusually light for a Friday night, and the cab circled the block three times before Isabella received the anticipated text message. This text came from Samantha, one of the more intimate staff members, and she'd given him a five-star rating, plus two devil emojis. That was a first, given Samantha's disdain for men. Isabella asked the driver to pull over when they were within walking distance of the bar. Parking at a distance was another security measure she had adopted to avoid anyone tracing the pick-up location of the cab. She handed over a sizeable tip and stepped out, still far from the bar. After less than a minute's walk, she had arrived and was greeted, as always, by Jake, the well-known-to-her mountain of a doorman at Riley's

Cocktail Bar. He let Isabella pass with a massive toothy white grin and a slight bow, holding the door open as she swept by. She reciprocated with a blown kiss. Every moment was streaming to her online members. A continuous flow of messages arrived on her device. She responded to the occasional request for a glimpse of this part or that part of her body. For the most part, her fans were happy to enjoy the view from Isabella's perspective. They called it Point Of View, or better still, POV.

Isabella dropped off her overgarments and large handbag at the cloakroom, keeping just a clutch bag with her, and then strode confidently into the main bar, although she had a slightly elevated heart rate. Whether or not she did this as part of the role, she still felt nervous whenever she met someone for the first time. The bar staff did a great job keeping two bar stools free on such nights. One for her guest and the other so she could slip in without any awkward standing up, sitting down moments. She scanned the row of similar-looking men lining the bar and noticed a couple of empty stools. Samantha, behind the bar, spotted Isabella enter and walked casually along the staff side of the bar until she stood directly opposite the right man. She sent Isabella a cheeky wink, raising her eyebrows as if to underline her first impression of him. Isabella returned her smile with her severest telling-off expression before giving her a big smile of appreciation. She made a beeline to the seat next to him, sliding silently into position. Samantha was with her moments later, a Porn Star cocktail, on the house, already ready and waiting for her arrival. Isabella discretely exchanged the drink for a button cam, which Samantha pinned to her top once she'd turned around to avoid prying eyes. She then took a second cam, placed it on the bar top, and slid it slowly towards the VIP sitting next to her. They had yet to acknowledge each other. The man swivelled slowly on his bar stool until he was diagonal to Isabella. He looked her directly in the eyes and gave away the merest hint of a smile. She returned his gaze.

"Hello, Isabella. I'm Zach. It's a pleasure to meet you in the flesh."

Oh, this one was very smooth! And Samantha hadn't exaggerated either. This man had everything, from his looks to his physique, tailored suit, expensive after-shave, and the sound of his voice. He was a rugged, fit, but not pumped up, 40-something, with dark, almost black hair, long enough to make him a contender for an old boyband, just the merest hint of stubble, a square jaw, and glinting eyes. Isabella felt a rare flush of lust between her thighs.

"Hello, Zach. Would you mind if I pin this camera to your lapel before we begin?"

Isabella reeled off the standard greeting whilst she felt her head spin a little, even though she hadn't touched a drop of alcohol all day. Zach leaned in toward her, returning the cam she'd placed in front of him a few seconds earlier. Isabella took this gesture as the first indication of his likely dominant male behaviour. She consented, as in her line of business, she was more likely to encounter dominant males, especially on BDSM nights like tonight. The button cam was pinned and patted into place before being activated with a pinch. She then opened her clutch, took out her phone, opened the app and checked that all three cameras were operational. Viewers could now choose three views or enable split screen mode to watch from every angle concurrently. There was a flurry of activity as a large proportion of the female audience and a few men messaged Isabella with various degrees of envy, lust, and general appreciation for Zach.

"It looks like you're getting the public vote", reeled off Isabella with a modest smile.

"Should I say thank you to your, sorry, to our audience?" responded Zach, with just a hint of playful sarcasm in his voice.

"You can say anything you like, Zach", came back the reply from

Isabella.

She put a little more stress on pronouncing his name. It helped reinforce the name in the minds of those listening. The more familiar he became to them, the more they invested in asking both of them, rather than just Isabella, to interact.

For the next twenty minutes, they engaged in a psychological game of arm wrestling, much to the delight of the paying audience, as each of them vied to gain the upper hand. Isabella sought to be the hotwife or femme fatale in this new yet fleeting relationship. On the other hand, Zach was determined to impose his dominance over Isabella, making her submissive to his masterful presence. Isabella found it refreshingly exciting to have to make an effort with a VIP, and Zach wasn't going to become the passive actor in this play. Meanwhile, Samantha had planted herself, with a pint glass and tea towel in each hand, directly opposite the two of them, wiping the glass to within an inch of its life. She was drawn increasingly into the fast-paced conversation and highly entertaining mating ritual before her very eyes. Even she was getting aroused by the whole thing, though she couldn't figure out whether it was Zach or Isabella getting her hot around the collar.

Eventually, they agreed that enough was enough and called it a stalemate. Samantha drew breath for the first time in who knows how long and decided to take a ten-minute toilet break with a glass of wine and her favourite mini vibrator. The ratings on her app were going through the roof. Isabella called time, and Zach paid their bar tag, hopped off the stool, and offered her his hand as she alighted beside him. Samantha turned off and returned the button cam to Isabella before sending her the most indiscreet wink you can imagine. They collected their coats and a large holdall that Zach had brought with him from the cloakroom before they made off together for their next, Club Inferno, in the heart of the Soho district of London.

CHAPTER THREE

The club was no more than a ten-minute walk, so they made their way on foot. Even after the sun had set a good half hour earlier, it was a warm evening. As only Isabella's button cam had sound enabled, her viewers got a clear audio-video feed without the echo you would find if both devices were recording and transmitting their conversation simultaneously. Isabella walked with her arm looped under Zach's and, to the casual passer-by, they looked like any other high-class couple taking an evening constitutional stroll through the streets of London. Only the privileged paying few were privy to their real intentions.

Whilst approaching their destination, an unexpected incident arose. A tall attractive brunette, probably in her early fifties, detached herself from her female companion and walked straight toward Isabella and Zach. She stopped right in front of them, blocking their passage. The woman looked Zach straight in the eyes, her own eyes blazing. She paused for a moment without saying a word, then slapped him forcefully on the cheek. His face hardly moved as he took the assault in his stride. Then, she leant forward, took his face in her hands and landed a long, passionate kiss on his lips. Once done, she released her grip on him, spun on her heels and walked back to the friend she'd abandoned just a few moments earlier. Zach shook his face ever so slightly, grimaced for the first time as the pain he'd been subjected to started to sink in, then offered his arm to Isabella again, and they set off in the same direction. Neither of them said a thing. Isabella had been surprised by the off-script events that had just occurred. For once, she was lost for words. Finally, Zach spoke.

"That was my ex-wife", was his only comment.

"Oh", responded Isabella, and the conversation ended as quickly as it had begun. The ratings soared once more.

A few minutes later, they arrived at Club Inferno, the Hell Club, an adults-only venue with very selective membership criteria. Isabella was a fully paid-up club ambassador, the highest-ranking membership you could achieve through a combination of money and attendance. It had taken her two years and countless visits to attain this level. They bypassed the waiting queue and were fast-tracked into the venue. A further cloakroom visit followed, although Zach chose this time to keep the holdall with him. They then passed through privacy velvet curtains into the main area. Isabella offered to show Zach around, but he declined gracefully, following her to where they would be seated.

An elevated stage central to the room offered their clientele non-stop erotic entertainment, from both men and women, performing staged sets with a BDSM theme running throughout. A long, well-furnished bar ran the length of one side of the venue. The main floor had large leather sofas scattered throughout, some against the walls, others paired together, facing each other for larger groups wishing to socialise. Dark metal cages suspended from the ceiling contained scantily clad men and women in leather and bondage gear. Most of the guests were well-heeled types from their mid-forties through the late sixties. The men wore suits, open-buttoned shirts, and copious amounts of after-shave. Women wore lace, leather or steampunk. One or more outlandish outfits consisted of thin strips of leather and a little more. Background music was provided by a trio discreetly tucked away in the far corner.

As a club ambassador, Isabella had a sofa and low table reserved close to the stage, and table service was available. The club also had an app for their members. The app allowed guests to order from the comfort of their seats. Guests could also select from one of the dozen or so servants available to do their bidding. Each one had an online profile and photo gallery, a brief biography, and their sexual tendencies and other vital intimate statistics. Isabella swiped left through the list until her eyes fell upon Chloe, a relatively new employee at the club. The profile showed a woman with flowing dark brown hair, deliciously pert breasts and infinitely longer legs than Isabella, wrapped in a minimal amount of leather, sufficient to maintain a degree of decorum. A moment of reflection, to make sure she'd made the right choice, she held up her phone for Zach to consider too. His nod of approval sealed the deal, and with a swift swipe right, they had booked Chloe to look after their every need for the evening.

The champagne and conversation flowed as Isabella and Zach settled into the ambience of Club Inferno. Over the next two hours, several couples, men and women, came by to introduce themselves. A few knew Isabella personally, and to her surprise, others recognised Zach. They even discovered they had a couple of mutual acquaintances. As the evening wore on, they relaxed together, watching the performers go through the motions of intimacy. They found themselves very much attuned to the other's emotions. They laughed out loud together when one of the acts took what they were doing a little too seriously, with an expression meant to transmit desire but looked more like an acute attack of gastroenteritis.

Their bodies crept closer as the minutes passed, with slight adjustments to their positions, invisible to all but the most attentive observer. Eventually, their thighs came into contact with the other. Their shoulders and legs followed. With the residual air gap gone, Isabella was as close as she'd ever been to a fully clothed random stranger. She felt at ease and had almost completely forgotten that she was still transmitting live on air to her increasingly female viewers. From behind their screens, dozens of her followers watched this blossoming romance evolve before their eyes.

Isabella had muted her speaker and so was oblivious to the messages appearing, one after the other, on her app. Her fans had coalesced into two main factions, those cheering her on from a romantic, sentimental point of view and others egging her on to raise the temperature. In the end, Isabella followed the middle ground between both camps. This was turning into something more than a business-driven casual date for Isabella, although she didn't recognise the signs just yet. As for Zach, something more profound and darker was already swirling in his mind.

CHAPTER FOUR

As the clock struck midnight, the trio of musicians stopped playing; the lights dimmed further, dry ice began to rise from the four corners of the room, and the mood music changed to something more profoundly guttural. The stage lighting was replaced with laser beams from the ceiling, high above, pulsating in rhythm with the background soundtrack. Then, from a trapdoor in the centre of the stage, the master of ceremonies, Mistress Moana, appeared, dressed in the most outlandish lace and metal steampunk outfit you could imagine. The look was completed by fishnet tights, a black leather horse crop, and a microphone. Although she was well over fifty years old, she had the looks of a woman in her early forties. Ample breasts were restrained rather than exaggerated, and her backside was perfectly rounded. She was the epitome of class in an equally sophisticated venue.

By this stage, Isabella had realised that Zach was, at the very least, a frequent attendee of the same club where she had been a long-time member. Yet, she'd never seen him there before and thought she knew most of the regulars. She still had a lot to learn. Mistress Moana began her well-rehearsed welcome speech as the club shifted gears from early evening socialising to the more intimate and personal part of the event.

"Ladies and gentlemen", she began. "I welcome you all to Club Inferno and to a night of fiery passion you will remember for a long time, or rather until the next time you visit us, which you will, I assure you."

Despite this being the same monologue that Isabella and Zach had heard many times before, it was the first time they were listening to it together. They pushed their bodies closer still, and Zach made the first intimate move of the evening, wrapping his arm around Isabella and resting it on the back of the sofa. He didn't make contact with her, but she noticed his gesture and moved closer still to him for a few moments more, as they both knew what was coming next.

"So, shall we begin?" continued Mistress Moana. She was engaging the audience now, as part of her bonus package was predicated on the number of returning customers.

"Please, could all ambassadors step forward and join me on stage? Now!" Her final words were commanding, and one of the rules of etiquette that ambassadors signed up to was that whatever the Mistress that evening commanded, they had to obey without delay.

Isabella put down her champagne flute, shifted on the sofa, and stood up, giving Zach one last look at what suddenly felt like loss before heading to join Mistress Moana and the other ambassadors on stage. As she walked off, she turned and mouthed to Zach to keep an eye on her clutch bag. He looked down at it, then back at Isabella, nodding his confirmation. For the first time in a long time, the short distance from where she'd been sitting to the steps leading up the stage felt like a long walk. She climbed the stairs and joined her colleagues, lining themselves up to either side of Moana, looking for all intents and purposes like the cast of a West End musical. Then, close enough to still make out the colour of his eyes, she saw Zach looking straight back at her. He leaned back further into the sofa, straightening his black trousers with the palms of his hands, before stretching both arms across the backrest, looking quite the man in control. She gave herself a mental wake-up call and regained her focus. She was the best at what came next, and tonight she was going to excel.

Once all the ambassadors had lined up, both men and women, Moana stepped forward, much as you would imagine a Sergeant Major to do with a line of soldiers. She placed the horse crop under her armpit and began her inspection, walking to the far end, away from Isabella. Just as she reached the start of the line-up, a young man with well-developed abs and dressed in little more than a tiny leather thong appeared from behind the row of ambassadors. He carried two heavy brass containers as his biceps tensed nicely to support the weight. His thong barely concealed the impressive package beneath, compounded by his arousal and evident for all to see. One by one, the Mistress inspected the ambassadors, presenting them by name to the audience. There followed a few seconds of anticipation as she delved with one hand, extracting a card from one container, then the other. One card carried the name of a single or paired couple of VIP guests. The second card described an activity. The rules of the game were quite simple. Having read both cards, the nominated guest or guests would come up to take possession of the ambassador. Then, as each VIP had previously selected one of the waiting staff to serve them, they would join the guest. Together they would return to their allocated seating area and wait for all the other ambassadors to be assigned.

One by one, the coupling continued, with names and activities called out by rote. Isabella felt her heart racing, despite this being only one of many occasions where she had taken to the stage and participated in what she considered one of the most exciting aspects of her professional career. She was waiting for two things. First, who would Zach have assigned? Second, who would be her new master? The light began to come on in her mind as the realisation dawned that she felt a personal attraction to Zach. She felt her skin flush with mild embarrassment as the thought grew and took hold of her. For the first time in her life, she didn't want to be here. But it was too late to back out now. She had to go through with it, even though she suddenly wanted to be anywhere but here. Then, the first moment she was dreading arrived.

Mistress Moana was two ambassadors away from Isabella when she heard Zach's name announced. He and Ilona, a twenty-something blonde beauty from Ukraine, were coupled. Zach rose from his seat, adjusted his jacket and walked to the foot of the stage. Ilona stepped forward, looking to all intents and purposes as if she'd won first prize in a beauty pageant. In Isabella's mind, her crown had been stolen. Ilona left the stage and slid her arm beneath Zach's just as Isabella had done a few hours earlier. They sat down on her sofa just as Chloe arrived with a tray carrying three more flutes of champagne. She served the glasses to both Zach and Ilona, reserving the third for herself, then removed the apron, which indicated she was one of the catering staff and deposited her firm butt cheeks beside Zach. He found himself caught between a Ukrainian blonde bombshell and a nubile brunette. Worse still, their designated activity was to satisfy their master's every whim. Isabella resigned herself to coming off second best that evening, which was disappointing, to say the least.

When Isabella's allocation came, Mistress Moana dipped her hand into the container. She searched for the card holding the next VIP guest, who would win Isabella's undivided attention. After several seconds, Moana took the unusual step of peering into the container. Then she raised the microphone to her mouth and laughed out loud.

"It seems we have run out of VIP guests for this evening!" she exclaimed, slightly tongue-in-cheek.

"There must be a football match on tonight", she continued, much to the crowd's amusement.

Though not unheard of, it was rare for this situation to arise, usually because there were too few ambassadors for the number of VIPS. In this case, there were still two of them on stage, Isabella and, next to her, the last standing ambassador, an attractive young man she'd socially met here on a couple of occasions. His name was Michael.

"Well, we all know what happens in these circumstances", came the follow-up line from Moana. "It's auction time, and it's now open to all our guests tonight."

Club Inferno had a pretty good track record for dealing with all kinds of risks, and in this case, they would pass from randomly allocating ambassadors to auctioning off the remaining ones. Tonight, that meant Isabella and Michael. Moana pulled the horse crop from under her arm and instantly transformed it into a makeshift gavel.

"Do I hear £500 for Isabella?" came the booming voice of the Mistress through the PA system.

A voice hidden away in the far recesses of the crowd called out with an offer of £100, raising a few isolated laughs. Then, the bidding war began, and within thirty seconds, an offer of £900 was on the table. Isabella had hoped against hope that Zach would raise his hand, but he just sat there, watching the offers fly out from the guests mainly seated behind him. She'd expected to fly First Class tonight, but now it looked like she would be fortunate to end up in Business Class and potentially finish in one of the Economy seats. The bidding slowed, with two remaining guests competing to outbid each other. Mistress Moana used the horse crop as a pointer, first in one direction, then the other, and then back again. Finally, a groan went up from the crowd as the best, and the final offer from an elderly couple in Business Class reached the heady heights of £1,300. The Economy class bidder shook her head and vanished into the shadows.

CHAPTER FIVE

"Going once", came the countdown announcement from Mistress Moana, followed by a long pause.

"Going twice" came the second toll of the bell of doom for Isabella.

She raised her horse crop, cum auctioneer gavel in the air, ready to slap it into her open hand to end the bidding and hand Isabella over to whatever whim or desire the elderly couple had in mind.

"£5,000" came a booming voice front and centre to the stage. It was Zach.

A collective gasp sounded around the room. Mistress Moana was taken aback.

"Did I hear you correctly? £5,000?" quizzed Moana.

Zach didn't respond, limiting himself to nodding slowly.

"Then it's £5000 for this beautiful specimen," Moana responded, quickly recovering from her momentary hesitation. "Do I hear any more?"

The couple on the cusp of owning Isabella shook their heads in disappointment. They had come so close to winning the auction to see it wrenched from their grasp at the last moment. A few seconds later, the makeshift gavel had fallen, and Isabella's very own VIP member had rescued her. The room burst into applause as Zach collected his ambassador. She couldn't resist whispering in his ear as he took her arm under his.

"You waited right to the end to do that! Now I understand why the ex-wife still loves and hates you."

He turned toward Isabella and greeted her for the first time since they'd met with a genuinely affectionate, if somewhat smug, smile."

"You're welcome", was all he came up with in response.

They reached the sofa where Chloe and Ilona were waiting. Zach gestured to Chloe, who moved over to make space for Isabella. The four of them sat together in silence for a while. Isabella had gone from feeling happy an hour ago to panic, and now she was feeling jealous, surrounded by unwelcome guests, interrupting the flow of the evening. Jealousy had replaced rational thought within the space of a few hours. Where had that confident entrepreneur gone? How was it possible that all it took were good looks, gentlemanly charm, and a bad-boy vibe? Isabella tried to shake off the feeling of desperation, but it had taken hold suddenly and unexpectedly. There was nothing she could do to break free of these emotions, or was there? In the ensuing silence, she came up with an all-or-nothing plan; the winner takes it all. She took a pen and paper from her bag and placed them in front of Zach.

"Okay, everyone", she began, "Let's see what Zach has planned for us".

She turned to him, smiling, and continued.

"I wonder what that naughty mind of yours can conjure up? I want to see how wild and passionate you can be. Shock me if you can."

The words came rushing out of her mouth almost without thinking. The two other women turned inwards, their mouths slightly ajar, as they suddenly became supporting actors to the two main protagonists. Zach paused to absorb the challenge Isabella had just laid down. But his expression changed as he realised what she was attempting to achieve.

"I thought you'd never asked", he quipped mischievously.

The bad boy look in his eyes took on a new level of wickedness. He leaned forward exactly as Isabella edged backwards, pushing herself deeper into the sofa. She'd thrown down the gauntlet, willing to bring her best game to the table. Zach had accepted the challenge. He picked up the pen and, after a brief moment of reflection, began writing. After less than a minute, he laid down the pen and carefully ripped the sheet into three equal parts.

"There are only two rules we all need to follow. First, don't read the note until it's your turn, and second, comply with instructions. Does everyone agree?"

He waited until all three consented to the rules. Then he folded the sheets and asked them to pick one each.

"Now, which one of you would like to go first?"

Isabella considered his question a moment and decided to wait it out. Ilona hesitated only a few seconds longer before raising her hand enthusiastically.

"Excellent. You two, please place your instructions on the table. Ilona, you can now read yours, hand it back to me, and begin."

Isabella and Chloe placed their unread instructions on the table, and Zach moved them across the table, out of reach. Ilona took a deep breath, unfolded hers and read it carefully. Isabella and Chloe watched as Ilona's eyes scanned the document. She paused for a second, then looked up and nodded, handing the sheet to Zach. Zach took the paper and tucked it away in his jacket. Ilona stood and moved in front of Zach, leaving him flanked by Chloe and Isabella. Ilona bent forward, wrapped her arms around his neck and gave him a long passionate kiss. Then she straightened, tugging Zach simultaneously and ordering him to stand. He followed her command dutifully, already anticipating which instructions she had received. Ilona shifted him sideways as he rose, gesturing that he should sit on the coffee table facing toward the now vacant space between the two women. He obeyed, and Ilona took his place between Chloe and Isabella. She fixed him in the eyes and blew a kiss in his direction, a wry smile crossing her lips as she did so. Isabella was watching Zach's reaction as Ilona made her first moves. He, instead, was focused on Ilona. The intensity of his gaze sent shivers through Isabella. She wanted him to look at her that way. At this point, Ilona paused, waiting for something to happen.

Around the club, the other VIP clients were similarly interacting with their ambassadors and assistant, whilst most clients were deep in conversation in small groups or were observing from nearby what was happening in the VIP section. Two younger men approached their sofa and, as club etiquette dictated, had stopped short of engaging with the group, limiting themselves to positions just behind the sofa. Zach noticed their arrival, although Isabella and the others had not.

Zach bent down and took the holdall he'd carried into the club. It was beneath the table, where he'd left it on their arrival. He unzipped it while Isabella and the others watched as he delved into the bag, searching for something. He first extracted two identical sets of blank and red handcuffs, followed by matching ankle spreader bars. Zach nodded in the direction of Ilona, who took her cue and stood once more. Then, in total silence, she proceeded to pick up the two sets of handcuffs, turning toward Isabella and Chloe. She bent down toward Chloe and ordered her to raise her wrists. Chloe obeyed, keeping her gaze on Zach as she did so. Her wrists were cuffed. Ilona checked them to make sure they were sufficiently tight and would not come loose. Once she was satisfied, she turned to Isabella and repeated her request. Isabella took a deep breath and offered up her wrists. She noticed Ilona had an enticing smile as she proceeded to bind her wrists. She tightened them just enough to make Isabella grimace for a moment. Ilona had no intention of giving Isabella a way out.

Next came the spreader bars. Ilona followed a similar procedure to the one she'd adopted for the handcuffs. This time, however, there was a slight twist. Before strapping the two women's ankles to the bars, Ilona kneeled in front of each of them, inviting them to raise their waists off the sofa. As they did so, she slipped her hands beneath their dresses and pulled down their underwear, removing them and handing them over to Zach. She then proceeded to tie their ankles. Isabella felt a little exposed as the fully extended bar was about a metre wide. They were both restrained. Throughout this exercise, Zach kept a close eye on the proceedings. Thoughts were rushing through Isabella's mind about his intentions and the instructions he'd given Ilona. It was only then that the true scale of Zach's darker, erotic side began to surface. The man undoubtedly had both controlling and voyeuristic tendencies, as both Chloe and Isabella were about to find out.

Zach raised his gaze, looking toward the two young men standing behind the sofa. Whether he'd orchestrated this moment or not, Isabella wasn't going to find out any time soon, but he clicked his fingers, and the two men immediately circled the sofa coming to a halt in front of the two bound women. Ilona moved in the opposite direction, finishing up where the two men had started, right behind the sofa. She leaned over and grabbed hold of the chains holding each pair of handcuffs. Then, with a forceful tug on both, she brought both women's wrists and arms up and over their heads. Now they found themselves restrained and gagged, with their arms taken out of service, being held firmly by Ilona, who stood firmly behind them. Isabella and Chloe were both feeling nervous but excited at the same time. They looked ahead, each one taking in the young man standing silently before them, whilst between those two, Zach sat looking at Isabella and Chloe with a burning desire in his eyes. Isabella felt the first flush of arousal. She expected Chloe would be feeling the same.

Seconds after Ilona had restrained them, the two men began unbuttoning their shirts. They did so in a way which made Isabella shiver excitedly. Both were fit, handsome and most likely at least ten years younger than her. Once unbuttoned, they kicked off their shoes. Neither of them wore socks. Then, just as Isabella expected them to continue undressing, they both fell to their knees. Isabella's mind raced, asking herself what they would do next. The answer arrived moments later as both men took a spreader bar in both hands and swiftly raised them above their heads, taking Isabella and Chloe's ankles and legs with them. Suddenly both women found themselves with their arms held up and back and their legs spread apart and on high. Isabella realised that from this position, her young man had the clearest of views between her legs. She tried to guess what was coming next but was only half right.

She fully expected the man kneeling before her, holding her legs, to lean forward and engage in one of her favourite pastimes, using his lips and tongue to pleasure her. In this regard, she was right. However, she hadn't anticipated that Zach would stand up and take hold of both spreader bars, lifting them even higher. This gave both men greater freedom to engage the women in a deliciously decadent few minutes of oral sex. Isabella let go of any residual nervousness as she felt strangely safe with Zach controlling events. Not only did she have the pleasure of being watched by Zach as this stranger aroused her, but mid-way through, the two men swapped places, and she could enjoy the two of them for the price of one. By the time Zach's arms began to drop, Isabella had gone close to going over the edge. Chloe, for her sins, had demonstrated even less resistance, soaking the sofa on two occasions, one for each of her unexpected lovers.

Eventually, both men pulled away, and Zach lowered his arms, releasing the bars as he did so. Their legs came back down to earth. Isabella was thinking that, despite her earlier feelings of jealousy, nervousness, annoyance and pretty much every other emotion she could have, she was now feeling warm, aroused, and enjoying the intensity of fulfilling Zach's darker fantasies. Thinking that Ilona had fulfilled Zach's first wish, she didn't expect what would come next. Instead of releasing both women from their bonds, the two men bundled Isabella and Chloe around on the sofa. They found themselves kneeling on the cushions, facing the back of the seat, with their ankles still spread apart and their butts now in the air. Surely, thought Isabella, there wasn't still more to come in this first fantasy of his.

Ilona took the opportunity to go a little off script as she still held tight on the two handcuffs. She lifted her dress just enough to slip one hand underneath and wriggle free of her underwear. With Chloe and Isabella held captive, their heads leaning over the back of the sofa, they were at the perfect height for what Ilona wanted to do. She approached Chloe, lifting the front of her dress and exposing herself right in front of Chloe's face. With a mix of surprise and lust, Isabella looked as Ilona pushed herself into Chloe's face, taking her head with her free hand and guiding Chloe to the place she wanted her to go. Both women groaned with pleasure as Chloe's tongue made contact with Ilona's dampness. Ilona began gyrating slowly, taking Chloe's tongue as far as she could.

Whilst this was going on, behind the scenes, the two young men had removed what remained of their clothes and were standing naked, one behind Isabella, the other behind Chloe. The first that Isabella knew was when she suddenly felt her backside making contact with something hard. She immediately realised what was happening. A glance over her shoulder toward Chloe confirmed her first impression as she saw the other man echoing what was happening to her. She watched as her companion groaned even more as he slowly drove his cock deep into her ass. Isabella could feel the same thing happening to her. She tried to relax as something substantial began to force itself inside her. Her butt muscles tensed despite her best attempts to control them, but despite that, he was hard enough to overcome any residual resistance her backside attempted. Moments later, she felt the entire length of his young cock deep inside her bottom. She had to give it to Zach; this was pretty impressive stuff.

As both men gradually increased the force and speed of their penetrations, Isabella found herself the centre of Ilona's attention. Having tired of playing with Chloe, Ilona moved over to Isabella and repeated her earlier actions. This time, however, she tried a slight variation on the theme. Ilona first raised one leg over the back of the sofa, and then the other ended up sitting on the backrest, with her feet planted to either side of Isabella. In this position, Isabella found herself face-deep in Ilona. This afforded both of them much easier access to Ilona's throbbing pussy. While she took a pounding in her young backside from the man's cock, she enjoyed the pleasure of Ilona soaking herself as Isabella lapped up the other woman's wet juices.

This continued for a few more minutes until both men had reached the point of no return. They slipped out from Isabella and Chloe and just made it in time to shift behind the sofa, from where they could feed our hungry mouths with their abundance of warm, tasty cum. The two women took as much as they could in their mouths before Ilona joined in, kissing both women and feeding her hunger for the men's cum. Zach remained where he'd been standing all along, a silent observer of his erotic fantasies playing out before him.

EPILOGUE

Although there had been enough excitement for one night, much more was to come. For Zach and Isabella, there was a new world they were about to discover together and two fantasies that still needed playing out. Those, however, are both stories for the next time

ACKNOWLEDGEMENTS

First and foremost, I want to thank my darling Isabella, aka P, for your willingness to read and critique my early drafts. This book would not have been possible if you hadn't been in my life. Tomorrow promises to be so much more exciting with you by my side. You are my muse and inspire me to be the best I can be.

Thanks also to those kindred spirits who joined us on our first tentative steps into the fascinating universe of this alternative lifestyle. We hope the good-looking ones will stick around; it promises to be a wild ride.

Finally, but equally importantly, I am grateful to you, the reader, who makes the effort of writing worthwhile by reading these stories, providing generous, preferably five-star feedback, including a 100-character review, and recommending this book to all of your friends.

M J Brooke

Printed in Great Britain
by Amazon

14949778R00142